D1528058

# A SECRET BROTHER'S VOW

KATE CONDIE

*To Michelle, for being my champion*

# 1

---

C hristian walked through his mother's home, empty of anything personal. No longer theirs, according to the bank. It felt wrong to sell it, as though he was selling his memories of her. But everything was tainted now. The omission of truth held the musty smell of old lies. He'd always known he was a bastard, but to learn his father had known of him, had been supporting them financially all these years, had been visiting her ... Christian straightened his fingers and stretched them in an attempt to not make a fist to swing at his father's face.

Francis Graham. Christian wished he'd never met Francis at that law office. He'd have been able to go the rest of his days never knowing the man, imagining whatever he wanted to about the old renegade. Nobody would have been able to prove him wrong.

But Christian wasn't a child anymore. Even if he had never met Francis, he wouldn't have continued lying to himself. When he really thought about it, he must have known someone had been paying for their every need. That *someone* had been his father. The thought might have soothed him in childhood. To know his father was alive and cared enough to provide them a comfortable life. Now Christian was an adult, providing for himself, and he had no need of the man. He clenched his jaw. Except, even Christian's ability to provide for his future was due to Francis's money. For without it, his mother would have never been able to afford Christian's schooling.

What was worse? A father who did nothing? Or a father who did everything except love his child?

Christian tugged the handle to the front door and shut it behind him with a soft click. The house was sold, his last day at this job done. Nothing kept him here anymore. He walked through the garden, dead from winter with brown dahlia stalks reaching for the sky as though begging for the warmth of summer to return. The front gate creaked as he went through it, as it did every winter. He wouldn't be the one to oil it come spring. It clanged shut behind him and he found he didn't much care who oiled it, or if they tore up the garden his mother had spent all her time planting. The garden had only been a distraction. Something to fill her time because a mistress had all the time, yet none of the friends.

Christian didn't turn back for a last look. He was done with that life of shame. He would move to the land in North Carolina that his aunt had purchased on his behalf, and he would never again think on the sadness of his childhood. But before he went east, he had to go west, just to see.

---

CHRISTIAN LET OUT a slow breath to settle his nerves and turned his attention to the open window and the many passengers on the platform saying goodbye to their loved ones. Children with both mothers *and* fathers. Happy marriages and couples who could be seen together. He moved to turn away but two women caught his eye with their swift embrace.The taller one stepped back and took the other by the shoulders, dipping her head so her eyes met the smaller one's tear-filled gaze.

Their voices carried through the steam that billowed from under the train. "You take care of yourself. If not for you, then for the babe. It's all you have now."

Christian leaned nearer to the glass. He clicked his tongue in pity. Such a young thing. Already widowed.

One of the women continued. "He'll visit." She cast a look over her shoulder then pulled her friend closer. "His wife may never have children, if you're lucky. This child could be his heir."

The window in front of Christian's mouth fogged at his slow exhale. She was no widow. Rather, a mistress. He almost laughed. One life lost, another gained. Here was a new mistress, stepping into the void that his mother had left.

The younger girl's lip trembled. She picked up her single valise and gave her friend a stiff nod. She walked along the train and Christian picked at his nails. Two bastards and a mistress leaving Chicago. Most chaplains would say a train housing such abominations would be cursed. Perhaps a wreck would be appropriate. Might it be better for the woman to die early than to live a life of shame followed by a lonesome death? In the end, only her garden had brought his mother comfort, and even it had died before she had drawn her last breath.

The train squealed and began a slow chug forward. Christian didn't want to die. He *had* many times in his life, but now wasn't one of them. He'd wondered why he had lived through infancy when so many children did not. If he hadn't been born, or lived to adulthood, his mother could have been unburdened by the shame of his existence. She could have created a better life for herself. She wouldn't have been shackled to Francis. She would have been free to marry.

He closed his eyes and leaned his head against the seat back. He imagined his mother, smiling, laughing, placing her hand on his head. It was hard to think she could have been happier. And yet, no woman could truly be happy living the way she had. In secret, in shame. He pressed his lids tighter and tried to block out the angry thoughts. The anger of his youth had ebbed, and she was gone. There was no point in remembering the hurt. Only the good. So he slowed his racing thoughts and let the train carry him, not to his mother's family in the Carolinas, but to his father's family in Montana. The family he never knew existed before that day in the law office. The brothers who had an inheritance just like his, but who were raised in the light instead of tucked away in a shadowy, country corner.

MELIORA CLOSED the door to her private cabin and let her head fall against the cushion on the back of the seat. Tears cascaded down her face. No longer could she hold them in, and what was the purpose anyway? She'd just said goodbye to her only friend and the woman was a paid servant of her uncle's household. As the train lurched forward she dropped her face into her hands, filling her palms with all the sadness she'd held back over the years.

All the times she'd stilled her chin or clamped her lips tight to hold in the cries. And all of it, for what? To be cast out in the end? Perhaps if she started now, the sobs would cease by the time she had to face another person. Luc had booked her a private cabin in the train, and for that she was grateful, but her gratitude ended there.

She hated the man, despised him, and yet, she wanted him to choose her. An angry hand brushed away the fat tear that came with that thought. Here she was once more, a burden being passed off to another. She should be used to it by now. Physically she was. She'd broken every important thing in her life down to fit into a single valise. There was no use in owning anything one couldn't carry. Not when that person moved as often as she. This didn't mean she wasn't traveling with baggage. She had two trunks filled with hats and clothes, all of which were purchased on her behalf with a glare and a week of resentment Meliora would just as well forget. Would she ever find a home? Or would the future be more of the same? Except now, her free hand—the one that didn't carry her suitcase—would hold the hand of a child.

She shook her head. It didn't matter. This child would have a mother to love her. The thought stuck in her throat. But childbirth was dangerous. What would happen if Meliora died like her mother?

When her tears were finally spent, Meliora pulled out her journal. She flipped past the pages of love notes she'd written back when she'd thought Luc a bachelor who might change her life forever. He had changed it, just not in the way she'd expected. She read over the instructions she'd written yesterday.

*In the event of my death, my child will go to Robert and his wife Carrie.*

She clicked her tongue, she'd forgotten to mention Robert's last name. She didn't have ink with her, nor would she trust using it on the train. She'd fix it when she arrived at the hotel tonight. She rested her head against the seat back and closed her eyes. Robert had been good to her—a little too good, or so his parents thought. His had been her first home after Father died from Typhoid. When her aunt and uncle feared the relationship she had with their son, they'd sent her on to an elderly aunt and uncle who didn't want a child and spent their time finding another suitable home for Meliora. And on and on through her family line until she'd reached the last uncle. His wife hadn't cared for Meliora. Their daughter, Hannah, cared for her even less, especially when Meliora outshined her in the classroom.

Despite her constant uprooting, Meliora did well in school, especially when it came to numbers. She liked the way she could count on numbers. Not like reading, where everything could have two or more meanings. No, that wouldn't do. Life should be calculable. If parents died, there should be a clear family to take on the orphan. And that family should call the new children their own, and there should be no option for pushing them onto another family. But wills are written in words and words are never clear.

Words. Luc told her words. Spoke promises that made her heart soar. If it were possible, Meliora would never speak again. She would let her actions speak for her. After all, who would believe a mistress who claimed she hadn't known the man was married? Especially when the man was as well-known as Luc Graham. She sighed. Who would believe a girl would be fool enough to give a man everything before she truly knew who he was? Who would have believed Hannah, when she told Mel that Luc was her only chance? That Hannah's parents were searching for a new home for Meliora and it would most likely be a workhouse. At least a workhouse was honest. Not like being skirted off to a country home far away from the wife of the man she'd trusted.

What was worse, Meliora couldn't even think of a time when Luc had *told* her he wasn't married. He'd paid her attention and flattered her. He'd called at the country house and nobody had said one word about his intentions. She knew now she'd been fed to the wolves by her very own family. Unable to find somewhere else for her to go, they'd encouraged Luc in his pursuit. They had played their cards well. For she was now Luc's problem and, as always, the solution to any problem was to stick Meliora on a train.

---

CHRISTIAN KEPT his seat while the other passengers disembarked. He had to wait for his horse to be unloaded from the stable car so there was no need to rush out the doors. He had taken just one step down the narrow hallway when a cabin door before him opened, and he caught it before it hit his face.

"Oh," came a feminine voice from the other side. "I'm sorry, I thought I was the last to exit."

He swung the door closed and found himself toe-to-toe with the same young woman he'd seen bid farewell to her friend. The woman who was no widow.

"Do you always come blasting out of cabins?" He opened the cabin door once more and looked inside. "Is there not a child with you?"

"I'm sorry. I thought the train was empty." The woman's eyes were tight and red-rimmed, and she stared at him with fear.

"As did I. Next time I'll keep my hands at the ready." He gestured toward the stairs that led out the door. "After you."

As though remembering her manners, she dropped her gaze and turned. He followed her down the stairs. His feet had just hit the brick platform when she stopped so abruptly he nearly collided with her. He shook his head at the foolish woman, stepped around her, and made his way to the stables. So she'd agreed to a life as a mistress and now she was afraid to walk any further? She'd figure it out. Women were much more capable than most men realized. It was only that men were usually around to take credit for everything the women do.

When he arrived at the stable he found his horse being led down the ramp. He approached the man who held the transport log and claimed his horse and equipment. Using a hitching post, he saddled his horse and climbed up. With a contented breath he turned his horse for town. He rode above the crowd, many of them in the faded plaids and calicos he expected this far west. He'd come from the country, but it wasn't wild like Montana. Rather, his home was a lush suburban countryside where the city folk came to get fresh air and the richest among them came to visit their mistresses. He searched the streets of Billings until he found a tavern and hitched his horse to a post near a window.

Stepping inside, he found a spot at the bar where he could see his horse. A buxom woman appeared with a flagon of beer. She set a mug down in front of him. "Drink?"

She leaned forward to pour, but Christian put his hand atop the vessel. "No, thank you. I'd like some food."

She rested the pitcher on her hip. "We've barley stew and bread."

He nodded. "That will be fine."

As the woman walked away he removed his hat and leaned into the back of the wooden chair. Too late to ride for the Graham's ranch tonight. He'd have to wait until the morning. His mind told him to buy a ticket east and forget this place. But his heart thudded with determination, and he knew he wouldn't turn back, no matter how logical.

## 2

Meliora waited on the train, unsure of how her face looked after so much time spent crying. She watched out the window until passengers thinned out and there was no longer any noise outside her cabin door. She gathered her valise and steeled herself for company. She noted the weight of the purse in her skirt pocket. It contained money as did the purse on her wrist. She also had more stored in the trunks of clothing. Her aunt had insisted she bring the clothes they'd bought her, saying Meliora's clothes were fit only for a runt and would not do for *their* daughter.

Meliora readied to deal with the station master and acquire a ride with her trunks to The Three Horses, which was apparently the only hotel Luc deemed safe enough. He was very clear on her travel instructions, though not so worried that he'd planned to accompany her. Perhaps he didn't mind too much if she were robbed and left for dead. With that angry thought she blasted through the cabin door, hitting something on the other side. A deep "oof" came from behind the heavy wood and Meliora stepped to the side, closing the door and revealing a tall man on the other side. She surveyed his face. Was he badly hurt?

After an awkward exchange where she was certain he knew of her shameful condition, she made her way off the train, but the moment her feet touched the platform she realized she was alone and far from anyone who could help her. The gravity of that loneliness settled in her feet, and she found she couldn't take another step.

Behind her, the man grunted, stepped to the side, and continued on his way. She watched his retreating form, wide in the shoulders and tense, as though he was angry with the whole world, or possibly just with her.

She stood in her spot, her mind spinning with Luc's instructions written on a note in her pocket. She reached inside and gave the paper a squeeze. She had no need to read it, for she had memorized every word. To her utter shame, she'd searched those words for any hint or promise of a future. But like the engine and cars behind her, she and her child were not to stay in this station forever. They would be moving along when the time came. She took one step forward and found that once she'd started, it was easier to continue.

She approached the station master. "Meliora Williams. I would like my trunks loaded into a wagon and a ride to The Three Horses."

The man surveyed her over his thin-rimmed circular glasses. "Wondered where you got off to. We had special instructions. Your things are in a coach." He jerked his head to the right. "Walk around the back. You'll see 'em. Come get me if you have any trouble."

"Thank you." She smiled, remembering she was alone and any friend was better than none.

Sure enough, behind the office was a weathered stage

coach that could have fit ten men. Her trunks were strapped to the back, and a man leaned against them, working something in his mouth. He spit a long spray of dark liquid, and Meliora shuddered, her stomach turning. She closed her eyes, her mouth filling with saliva the way it did when she was about to be sick. *Not now.* She pictured the thick forests of trees she had passed during her train ride, imagined the fresh air that would be in those forests, and pretended she was breathing it in rather than the dusty air of this cowboy town.

When the threat of being sick passed, she approached the man. "Are you the driver of this coach?"

He ran his gaze down the length of her. "Yes, ma'am. Clive Clark. And you must be Ms. Meliora Williams."

She nodded and he tugged the door open. Just as she passed she saw him turn his face and she sucked in a loud breath so she wouldn't hear the sound of his spit hitting the dirt.

Once inside, she surveyed the upholstery. It wasn't nearly as bad looking inside. It seemed the Montana sun and snow aged the outside more than passengers had aged the inside. Such was the opposite of her. Mel was worn ragged on the inside, but outside she was everything a lady should be. Her hair was tended. Her face youthful. Her clothing expensive. Yet, what was the point of it all? She was ruined. A disgrace. Her aunt's words rang in her head. *You should be glad your father died before he saw you brought so low.*

Mel closed her eyes against the memory. She wished she could be hit on the head, like that neighbor who forgot everyone, even her own husband and children, only remembering her childhood. It was the oddest thing, yet to Meliora it was lucky. If only the past could be taken from her, Mel might be happy. She might be allowed to carve out a new life, one made by her own hand and not the hand of others. But she'd like to keep her memories of Mother and Father. She'd endure anything to keep those memories with her.

She touched the locket that held both her mother's and her father's hair. Braided together, one for eternity. She pressed it open and stared at her mother's dark hair, so unlike her own. Her hair resembled her father's, which was much lighter and more dull. She'd never known him to have a full head of it.

The coach pulled to a stop and the door opened once more to reveal the steps of an inn. It was well lit and the paint was clean, not peeling like the other buildings on the street.

A round man with a laughing smile stepped through the entry and smiled at her, a silent laugh on his lips. "Welcome, Ms. Williams. We are pleased to have you at our establishment." He scooped her valise from her hands and gave a quick word and nod to the driver of the coach, who unbuckled Mel's luggage.

"Right this way." The inn owner smiled and led the way deeper into the building.

There were a few tables, all with crisp white table cloths and candlesticks lit against the setting sun. Mel might have been impressed if this wasn't what she'd grown up with. Money had never been lacking, but everything else had been. The corners of her mouth slid down. Some things would always stay the same. She should stop hoping for more. It seemed the fates had decided how her life would be. Whether it be one set of relatives or the next, one manor for another, or even a man who proclaimed his love then took it away in an instant, she would always live in comfort, but never be truly loved or wanted. Perhaps she should stop blaming the world, and realize the fault lay in the common denominator—her.

---

MORNING CAME TOO SOON, and as the innkeeper led her through the front door, Mel braced herself for the same coach driver as last night. Instead she saw two young men, dressed shabbily, but cleanly, standing in front of a coach that nearly glittered with its newness. They smiled, and they didn't have the same lump in their cheeks that spoke to the habit of chewing tobacco.

One turned to her and tipped his hat. "Morning, Miss."

She nodded and waited while the other man and the innkeeper wrestled her things onto the back. Such a nuisance. She wondered if it might do to tell the innkeeper to keep one of the bulky trunks and give the clothing to someone in need. Only she wasn't sure which trunk held the money Luc had sent, and she was only just realizing how very alone she was. That money was a comfort, even if it did come with too many gowns and two large trunks being moved from place to place. When the innkeeper had finished, he glared at the other man— the one who had first greeted her. "Get her door, son."

The young man jumped to obey, and Meliora had to bite her lips to keep from laughing. She climbed inside and at once was transported back to her aunt and uncle's home. The benches were covered with thick damask, and the wood was rubbed smooth. Either this coach was rarely used, or she was among the first of its passengers.

The ride was long and Meliora had to stop twice to be

sick. The young men offered to stop for the night and allow her a day's rest. She couldn't tell them hers was a sickness that would take longer than a night to cure. More like seven more months. Instead she insisted they continue and they looked at her with admiration she didn't deserve. Had she truly been ill, she would have begged them to stop.

By the time they reached their destination, Mel's body ached from the jostling dirt road and she felt fatigued from the lack of food in her stomach. She had too little energy to fear what would come next. So when the door opened, and she blinked into the setting sun, taking in the man ready to help her down from the coach, she almost lost her stomach again. He looked much too similar to Luc Graham.

# 3

U pon further inspection she realized it was not Luc but undoubtedly his brother. The two shared the same nose and strong jawline, but this man's face was hard. Nothing like the charming expression Luc always wore.

"Meliora Williams?" His voice fell deep and expressionless.

She nodded. The way he said her name sounded like a reprimand. She wouldn't be able to stand if this man called her Meliora the way her uncle had. Nor would she be able to stand if he spoke it in a gentler tone the way Luc had. "Please, call me Mel."

He stuck his hand out. "I'm Bastien Graham. Welcome to Aster Ridge."

He took her hand and gave it a firm shake before releasing it and lifting her bag from the grass. "Follow me."

Apprehension filled her belly as she did his bidding. She hadn't asked what the duration of her stay would be. Was Luc planning to keep her here until the baby came?

Longer? She gulped as she followed Bastien into the house. They entered the kitchen where a beautiful woman with a round belly stood, a frown on her face.

Bastien stopped and set Mel's bag on the ground. "Della, this is Meliora Williams." He turned to Mel. "This is my wife, Della."

Mel dipped her head. "Pleased to make your acquaintance."

Della held Mel's gaze for a moment before saying, "Yes, dear. Let me show you to your room."

Della moved quickly, apparently unperturbed by her giant stomach. Mel scooped up her bag and followed. She couldn't help but see her own future as she watched Della. It was probably best she was far away from Luc. He could remember her as the trim woman she'd been. If her maid was right, he might return to Mel one day. For marriage if his wife died, or for inheritance if his wife never had children of her own.

Della opened a bedroom door and stepped inside. "It's small, but the guest house is full at the moment."

The afternoon sun filtered through the lace curtains, lighting the faded quilt and pillows. "It's lovely. Thank you."

"Dinner is at seven. I'll ring the bell."

With a click, the door closed and Mel was left to herself once more. She sat on the bed, breathing in the scent of lavender and rosemary. The vase by the bedside was filled with both herbs. She leaned over and ran her hand along the rosemary stem, releasing more of the smell into the room and coating her fingertips with the scent.

Della hadn't been happy to see her. That much was clear. Did she think Mel a seductress who would set her sights on Bastien next? Would any wife believe Mel hadn't known Luc's wedded state? She shook her head. Mel had lived with enough families to know they stuck together. Somehow Luc would be the innocent and Mel the devil.

Well, that was fine. It had been years since Mel was loved. If there was one thing she'd learned since her parents' death it was that she didn't need love or acceptance. She needed food and shelter. Anything else only meant it would be harder to pick up and leave when it was time.

Mel poured a bit of water into the basin and washed her face. She used the looking glass to tidy her hair, and when she deemed herself appropriate, she joined Della in the kitchen.

Only it wasn't Della at the stove, but a petite blonde girl.

"Can I help?" Mel asked above the sound of something metal scraping the pot.

The girl turned around. "Oh, hello." She smiled, a warm greeting that made Mel sure this girl didn't know about Mel's condition nor her association with the Grahams. "No need to help. I believe Della is out at the guest house with Lydia."

If Mel were family she would know who this Lydia was. No doubt the girl assumed as much. "I'll find her later. I've been sitting all day, and I'd love to help with dinner. Can I set the table?"

The girl shot Mel a smile, her eyebrows raised in appreciation. "Sure."

Mel gathered plates from the shelf. "I'm Mel Williams."

"Fay Morris. Pleased to meet you."

Morris. Perhaps she was hired help. Despite being an

orphan, Mel had never learned much beyond needlework and painting. Whatever would come next for Mel, she might benefit from becoming this girl's friend and learning a thing or two in the kitchen.

Mel finished setting the table and watched as Fay worked, setting out bowls of greens and pouring gravy on top. The smell was heavenly, but just as quickly Mel's stomach turned, and she rushed for the front door. She heaved her lunch behind a rose bush and came up, wiping her mouth with the heel of her hand. When she turned, she saw Della and another woman walking toward her.

She straightened her back and hid her shaking hand in her skirts. She tried for a smile, but she knew her face shone with sweat.

Della's eyes ran down her frame in a way that told Mel she didn't miss much. "Meliora, this is Lydia. She and her family live in the guest house."

Mel dipped her head in acknowledgement, all she could offer when her head still spun.

Lydia stepped forward and placed a hand on Mel's arm. "When did you start feeling sick?"

No secrets in *this* family. Mel sighed. "A few weeks ago, and please, call me Mel."

"Mel, I'm glad you're here. I'm sure you're tired and sick, but if you ever feel well enough, we've much to do. My husband runs a ranch out here and believe it or not, the times when the guests aren't here are the busiest."

"I'm happy to help." She swallowed through the acid taste on her tongue and glanced at the mess in the dirt. "I'm sorry."

Lydia flicked her wrist. "Don't be. You made it outside. That's a sight better than some." She glanced at Della.

Della returned Lydia's look with a small smile that spoke of shared memories. Mel's heart twitched, as though mourning the loss of Hannah. Foolish as it was, Hannah had been the closest thing Mel had to a sister. Some of the time they had even laughed and enjoyed one another. But those times were rare, and there would be no chance to relive them. Mel was shamed, and no woman of class would publicly associate with such.

---

CHRISTIAN RODE through the valley until he found the house described by the innkeeper in Dragonfly Creek. A man was working on the fence. He straightened, lifting his hand to shield the sun as he squinted at Christian. He started forward.

Christian slid from his saddle to meet the man's outstretched hand.

"Willem Graham," the man said. "What brings you to our valley?"

Christian's words stuck in his throat like a burr in his horse's tail. This was his half-brother. He shook off the shock and spoke the words he'd practiced during his journey. "Christian Milnes. I heard there was a gentleman's ranch out here."

Willem glanced over his shoulder at the ranch house. "There sure is. Only, we're between groups at the moment. Are you looking to book a visit?"

Christian gave a laugh he hoped sounded casual. "I just wanted a tour. I purchased a bit of land back east, and I'd like to see what you do to make this a place men recommend to others."

Willem dipped his head. "Do they really recommend it?" His words were coated in humility and self-doubt.

Christian laughed and instantly hated himself for liking the man. Of course Willem was charming. He'd lived a charming life with everything a person could ever want.

Willem straightened. "You from Chicago, then?"

Christian bobbed his head to the side. "I'm from Aurora, but I was just in the city for business before I left for North Carolina." The business of meeting their father and accepting an inheritance. Christian's heart thrummed in his ears. Coming here had been foolish. This man resembled himself. Any stranger might point out that they were brothers. Did he truly dare to go any further? To meet more of this family he'd always wanted but never knew existed? This family who lived in the open, recognized and accepted.

That hard thought pushed his next words from his lips. "What do you say? Care to give me a tour?"

Willem eyed Christian and nodded. "Sure. You'll have to wait until the morning though." He glanced at the setting sun. "Dinner will be on soon. You're lucky. The bunkhouse is empty while we prepare for the next round of guests." He glanced at Christian's saddle bags. "Is that all you brought?"

Christian shrugged. "I travel light." Especially when everything he owned had already been sent to North Carolina.

Willem waved Christian toward the house. "C'mon, let's tell them there will be one more at the table tonight."

WHEN EVERYONE GATHERED for dinner Mel stayed out of the way and watched the bustling household interact. She noted which children belonged to whom. The mothering was done by all, Della chiding Lydia's boy, Milo, for dipping his finger in the gravy and Lydia helping Della's little girl into her seat.

A clanging sounded outside and Mel guessed that was the sign for dinner.

Lydia touched her shoulder. "Have a seat." Mel did and Lydia sat down next to her. "It gets a bit wild when everyone is inside. Just pray we don't have any more snow. It's the only way you'll make it out alive."

Mel couldn't help but smile. The house did feel like it was bursting, but there was *something* about all the bustle and the children and the love they all shared. Mel might even pray for snow just to see what it would be like to be cooped up with this rowdy bunch.

Bastien came in and kissed his wife then took his seat at the head of the table. Shortly after, deep male voices carried into the kitchen and two tall men with matching dark features came around the corner. Mel squinted at one of them for a moment. He was familiar, and she tried to place the features.

Lydia nudged her. "The one with the freckles is my husband, Willem."

Willem smiled at Lydia then addressed the room. "This is Christian Milnes. He'll be staying in the bunkhouse for the night." Willem grabbed a green bean from a serving dish that sat on the counter and pointed it at Bastien. "He heard of the success of my enterprise and wants to see how we do it." He stuffed the bean into his mouth and smiled as he chewed.

He walked over and leaned in to kiss Lydia on the forehead. "It smells wonderful, dear."

Lydia shook her head. "Tonight's dinner was Fay and Della. Our daughter has been giving me grief."

Willem turned to little Briget with one eyebrow cocked. "Are you going to have to labor in the field with me tomorrow?"

"Yes." She said in her tiny lisping voice, grinning as though the punishment was nothing of the sort. The table laughed and Willem shrugged at Lydia as though he was out of ideas.

Soon everyone was seated and the guest, Christian, sat next to Della with a shy smile. He turned away, as though embarrassed by her proximity. When he did, his gaze met Mel's.

Her breath left in a whoosh as she remembered him from the train. "You?"

"Ah," he laughed. "I didn't expect to see you again. Christian Milnes." He offered his hand, but his stare was hard and unnerving.

She gulped and took his hand. "Mel Williams. Pleased to meet you." Though she couldn't decide why she wasn't at all pleased to see him again.

Della's narrow gaze moved between Mel and Christian. "You two know one another?"

No doubt Della thought Mel was a floozy and this man was one of her customers.

Mel gulped, knowing any words she spoke would not be believed. "We took the same train. We weren't even properly introduced until now."

"Ah." Della's guarded expression said she was unconvinced.

Willem slapped the table. "You rode all the way from Billings? You must be starved."

With that, grace was said and silence rang on the subject of Mel and Christian's familiarity, though no doubt it was on more than just Mel's mind.

Bastien cleared his throat. "No Ivete?"

Della shook her head as she dished a bit of food onto her plate. "She's been very distant. I wonder how she likes living so far away from everyone."

Bastien pushed his lips out in a thoughtful pout. "I'd guess if she missed us she might join us for dinner when invited. I'll speak to Thomas."

Della brushed his arm with her fingertips. "I'm sure they have their reasons. After all, they did not promise to come whenever we called."

Bastien didn't say more, but his face said the matter wasn't settled. She tried not to stare, but Bastien looked so like Luc it was unnerving. If she'd arrived in the dark of night she would have surely mistaken him for Luc, and only a candle near his face would have convinced her otherwise.

She surveyed Willem next. He also shared certain similarities with Luc, but his face was sweeter, always smiling and not hard like his brothers' faces. What had so attracted her to Luc? He was hard like Bastien but had a charm about him like Willem. If he had more of Bastien in him and less of Willem, she would have been too frightened to fall for him.

As her gaze swept the company she longed to meet this Ivete ... a sister to these brothers, perhaps? Did she have that same square Graham jawline? She looked at Christian and even *he* seemed to resemble a Graham.

With a blink she shook her head. She was getting carried away and soon everyone would look like they were related. It must be the family atmosphere turning her head.

When the meal was through, the women stood and began clearing the plates and food. Bastien gestured Christian to take Della's empty seat, and the men talked while the children sat on their laps and the women washed and dried dishes.

Mel accepted a dish from Lydia. "Do you always eat together like this?"

Lydia shook her head. "The guest house has a small kitchen, but sometimes it's easier to make one big meal."

Mel passed the dry dish to Della who didn't meet her eyes. She moved away and placed the plate on the shelf. When she returned she kept her gaze anywhere but on Mel. "So, you met Christian on the train?"

Mel picked at her nails as she waited for the next clean dish. "I almost hit him with my cabin door. He was gracious not to mention it."

"Gracious indeed." Lydia quirked a brow and Mel couldn't tell if Lydia was teasing or thought Mel a liar.

Fay came around the corner with a pot filled with water. She rushed to set it atop the stove. "Oh, my. You all should be sitting with the men. I'm sorry ... Otto ... Well, he had a bit of news."

Della and Lydia pressed closer, clearly interested in whatever news Fay brought. Mel didn't know this Otto so she shrank against the counter and took up Lydia's place washing the dishes. At the first try she dipped her cuff into the water. She wrung it out and kept working while listening with one ear to what Fay was saying.

"He's got it in his mind to join Eloise in Oregon. Aaron

says he'll get Otto a bit of land and help him set up an orchard."

Della spoke. "I guess we couldn't expect him to stay forever. But what about your pa?"

"Who knows." Fay gave an irritated grunt. "Otto doesn't care to stay and find out."

Lydia said, "I'm sure it's not that. But he's a man now. He has to make his own way."

"He's barely a man, and Hugh and Lachlan didn't abandon us."

There was silence for a beat. Only the sounds of the men's conversation filled the room.

Lydia joined Mel, drying the dishes she'd washed.

Della patted Fay's hand. "I'm sure everything will work out."

Fay sighed. "I'm just going to leave these beans to soak overnight." She sidled up to Mel with a wink. "Let me finish these."

Mel lifted a shoulder and let it drop. "I don't mind."

Della said, "We can finish up here. See you tomorrow."

Fay smiled at Mel before turning to go. At least she had one friend, and it wasn't that man from the train. He'd been the last person she saw on the train. It made her feel as though he'd abandoned her to her fate. Ridiculous thought, but thinking clearly had been a problem as of late.

She glanced at her flat stomach. She wasn't alone. Possibly she never would be again. That thought brought her comfort as well as a slice of fear. What if the baby didn't love her? What if she was truly unlovable and she—not her family—had been the problem all along?

# 4

Christian lay in a bunk with inky black around him. Willem and Bastien hadn't stayed. They'd only shown him around the space then bid him goodnight. They were light —funny even— and he hated it. They had a home filled with children and beautiful wives. And the mistress, Mel, had been an interesting addition. He closed his eyes and recalled seeing her at the train station. The friend she'd been with wasn't here now, and she'd been alone in the cabin. No child with her. Perhaps the child was yet unborn, and she was too early to show any signs of the babe within.

What was she doing here? Did the rest of the Grahams know of her condition? Was she carrying Francis's child, or perhaps Luc's? It was all very Grecian tragedy to think of a woman —young enough to be his own lover— having been with his father, bearing a child that would be his half-brother. Her face swam in his memory, wide and scared on the train, then confused and a bit put out when she saw him here. She didn't show the forwardness he expected from such a woman. She was quiet, shy almost, as if she wanted to blend into the background. He wondered if that was how his own mother had been. She hadn't been some lustful woman throwing herself at men. She had been quiet and poised and proud. Despite everything, she had kept her head high.

Was Mel the same? He couldn't resent her like some would. He knew the future she had in store, and he could only pity her. If her child was a girl, it might fare better than a boy. A girl didn't need a last name. She could marry, and he knew better than most that men often didn't care about a woman's social standing. If she was beautiful, that was enough. If it was a girl, and if she looked anything like Mel, there would be no problem finding her a good husband.

He closed his eyes, trying to quiet his thoughts. As he'd rode here from Billings, the cold had gotten the better of him. He'd stopped for over an hour, trying to warm up then gain the momentum to leave again into the cold. He supposed even if he'd gotten here sooner they would have insisted he stay the night. At least he wasn't sleeping in their homes. He'd much rather stay out here, alone in the bunkhouse.

He thought about the house in North Carolina. He'd sent his aunt the money, and she claimed there was a bit of furniture she wanted to buy for it. Thanks to Francis, Christian had plenty of money for such luxuries, but he wouldn't have minded living in something as basic as this bunkhouse. He didn't need finery. He almost chuckled at the thought of his inheritance. Surely, if Francis had thought Christian would come here and would be laying in Willem's bunkhouse, he would do everything in his power to revoke that inheritance. Christian wasn't here to ruin anything for Francis. He only wanted to meet this family. He'd always wanted siblings. Maybe brothers to wrestle with or to teach him to fight or a younger sister to protect. He smiled into the dark. The need for siblings was gone. He'd learned to fight on his own, and Ivete was already grown and married. Any protection she may need was done by her husband.

That thought weighed in his heart with an unexpected heaviness. Ridiculous. She likely hadn't needed protecting, and if she had, she had three older brothers who would have pummeled anyone who thought to cause her harm. Maybe this was a foolish idea. Coming here only sharpened the pain of the revelation of his father's identity. He should leave. Tonight. Hop on a train east and care for his aunt and her family. Protect his cousins, teach *them* to fight. He would never gain the life he had lost through no fault of his own. Forward was the only way to go. He'd met two of his four half-siblings. That would have to be enough. One day in their presence wasn't so long. He could forget them. Forget Francis. Forget everything. He could put his parentage behind him. Find a wife of his own and bear legitimate children.

With a pang he remembered Mel embracing her friend. It was happening again. A single generation later. One more relative he would never meet.

---

CHRISTIAN WOKE in the morning to the warm smell of coffee and a note.

*Breakfast will be in the main house this morning.*

He sipped the still-steaming beverage and closed his eyes. It was thick and rich, better than any coffee he'd ever had before. Did Willem use his own money for such luxuries, or did the funds from his guests pay for this?

He dressed and walked across the prairie toward the main house. Its clapboard sides were unassuming. Even with the acreage and all the horses, one wouldn't know this house belonged to one of the wealthiest families in Chicago.

As he neared the house he heard a small cry. Turning, he saw a figure in the chicken coop. The skirts told him it was a woman, and only when he drew closer did he see it was Mel.

He dipped his face below the boxes. "Everything all right in here?"

Mel shook her skirts at a red hen. "It's filthy, and they keep coming at me."

Christian laughed and walked around, opening the door. "Do you have any feed?"

She shook her head then walked backward as the same hen came at her again.

"They think you have food for them." He walked forward and picked up the hen, holding it against his side like a saddle bag. "She's not going to hurt you." He glanced at the nesting boxes. "Go ahead." He pointed at a black chicken, down the way a bit, camouflaged as it sat in its shadowy box. "Be careful of that one."

But just as he said it, she reached in and touched the hen.

She let out a scream.

He moved toward her, and the chicken in his arm must have sensed him softening his hold. It flapped wildly and freed itself from his grip. It landed on Mel's skirts, and in her haste to get away from it, she tripped over the water trough and fell against the coop wall.

Christian shooed the red hen away with his boot. It hurried off in a rush of feathers that filled the small space. He offered Mel a hand.

She glared up at him. "I think you made everything worse."

Christian laughed. "No doubt I did."

She tried to rise but glanced over her shoulder. "Wait, I'm caught."

Chicken wire snagged the lace trim on her dress. Christian knelt at her side and unhooked each delicate loop from the stiff and rusty wires of the coop. As he worked, he longed to use his position to press her with questions about her condition and what she was doing here. But too soon he had freed her, and she was brushing filth from her skirts.

Christian reached up under the black chicken and found two eggs. He walked along the nesting boxes and found a few more, holding them in his free hand. When he was satisfied they'd found all the eggs, he lifted Mel's basket from where she'd dropped it in her fall and set the eggs inside. When the basket was off the ground, it revealed the runny center of a broken egg. The chickens rushed to eat it, and therefore rushed Mel.

She yelped and tucked herself behind him.

He laughed over his shoulder, then turned. "They are rather skittish, but I'd say you have that in common. They aren't going to hurt you. It's the rooster you need to watch for, and I haven't seen or heard one yet."

Mel undid the latch and stepped out, holding her skirts so they didn't get snagged the way her back had. He could see a loose thread on her lace from when he'd untangled her. He stepped through and watched the thread waving in the cold air. He couldn't help but watch it, alone and apart from the others, waving in desperation. His mother had enjoyed making lace and Christian knew enough to know if that strand was left exposed it would fray. It needed to be tied off and tucked away or it would ruin the entire length of lace trim.

When she was done with the door, he offered her the basket.

She shook her head. "I'm not taking credit for them. You're the gatherer here."

He shook the basket at her. "You went to great expense to gather these eggs." He looked pointedly at the lace along her shoulder. "Your dress will need some attention due to the adventure."

She twisted, as though trying to see the damage.

"It isn't bad." He pressed the basket into her hands. She took it, and he stepped around her to open the front door. He let her pass first then followed her into the kitchen.

Willem stood from the table and gave Christian a wide smile. "Glad to see you. Help yourself to breakfast. We'll want to get an early start. My wife says it will rain, and she is never wrong."

Christian nodded and helped himself to the buffet of food.

Willem sidled up to him and dished more onto his own plate. "So, tell me. Who told you about my enterprise?"

Christian found a seat at the table. "I don't know his name. He hadn't been here though, just said it was here."

Willem screwed up his face in thought. "I wonder why he hasn't booked a week." He turned to Bastien. "Am I making it too difficult to come out?"

Bastien clapped Willem on the shoulder. "Did he *recommend* the place?"

Christian shook his head. "My banker, Mr. Wright, told me it was a keen enterprise. Said you were an investor to watch."

Willem laughed. "I never knew Wright liked me so. That's quite a compliment. He's helped with a few of my investments. Good man. I'll pay him a visit next time I'm in town."

Christian nodded into his plate.

Willem boomed, "Bastien, you hear that? Wright recommended me as an investor to watch."

Bastien lifted his daughter from her chair and set her on his shoulders, then set his sights on Christian. "I wish you hadn't told him. Now we'll never hear the end of it. Wright likely meant to say mine or Luc's name instead." Christian wanted to laugh at their easy banter. How Bastien could cut his brother down, yet Willem hardly noticed.

Willem smirked at his brother then leaned closer to Christian. "Any questions before we embark on our tour?"

"What was your first investment?"

Willem leaned back and grinned. "That one was easy. I was only helping a friend."

Bastien set his daughter down and sat next to Christian. "He means the woman who owned the bakery. She was only *friends* with him because he was her best customer."

Willem chortled. "But friends nonetheless." He turned back to Christian. "Her husband died, and she had a young daughter. The bakery was new, and they hadn't yet turned a profit. Without his money it would have gone

33

under. I knew they would succeed, given enough time, so I invested. Now it's Archer's Bakery on seventh."

Christian raised his brows. He'd been there more than once during his brief stay in Chicago. He remembered the harsh woman who ran the place but also the pretty young woman who served pastries and took payment.

Willem raised a finger. "Even better, the daughter, Edna Archer, she's coming here" —he pressed his finger into the table—"to work for me. She'll be here next week."

Bastien leaned his elbows on the table top. "That worked out for you, but I don't think helping friends is always the right choice."

Willem leveled a look at Bastien. "You mean like when you went into this ranch with Thomas fifty-fifty?" He scoffed. "Helping friends is the benefit of having money." Willem sucked in a breath as though he'd said too much. He stared at Christian. What was he thinking? Did he wonder if Christian had the funds to start such an enterprise?

"I have a bit, I just received an unexpected inheritance."

Willem leaned close to Christian and cocked a brow. "Unexpected? Those are the best kind. Was it an uncle?"

Christian choked and coughed. "No. A family friend." Though he'd practiced these lies before he arrived, he struggled to keep his voice level. Talking with his half-brothers about his inheritance was surreal and a prospect he'd hoped to avoid. Now he was eating breakfast with these two men and found they were utterly and irritatingly enjoyable.

"I better check on my horse." Christian left before they could level him with any more questions.

Of course they were charming. They had perfect lives,

perfect childhoods. There was no need to prove themselves to anyone. No need to make a name for themselves. He rushed to the stables and walked through the aisle, past his horse and around the back. A sniff came from his left, and he turned to find Mel with her back to him, leaning on the fence. Her shoulders shook with each whimper.

Christian cleared his throat, and she spun, wiping her face.

"Are you okay?" The question was dumb, but he didn't have other words. Seeing her face now, made him realize she'd been crying on the train. Perhaps that was why she'd waited to be the last to disembark. Her eyes were puffy and her nose red and swollen. He took a step closer, but she turned away with a great sniff.

He joined her, leaning his arms along the same rail. Across the corral a barncat walked along the railing. "D'you think if I caught that cat and locked him in the bunkhouse, he'd catch the mouse that kept me up last night?"

She chuckled, but the end of it was too breathy to be a true laugh.

He shrugged. "Perhaps a cat is easier to catch than a mouse. Bigger, at least."

She slid her gaze to look sideways at him, watching him with a wariness that challenged him. She cleared her throat. "Are you here for your horse? I saw you on it in Billings. It's a fine mount."

Christian smiled. "Are you a horsewoman?"

She sniffed. "No. I'm one of those women who has dabbled in everything, yet I'm not proficient in anything of use."

He turned back to the corral and watched a horse

graze in the pasture beyond. "I'm not sure being a horse-woman is of any real use. What would you *like* to be proficient in?"

She pressed away from the fence. "I should get back." She moved to go, but stopped and turned her head to look over her shoulder so he could only see her profile. "Please don't tell anyone I was crying. I ... don't want to worry them over nothing."

"As you wish." He watched her go, her shoulders drooping and not even when she'd been crying did she look so pitiful as she did walking away.

He took her place, leaning his arms on the fence rail, thinking of his mother. Where had she gone when she carried him in her womb? Did Francis send her to some country estate like this? It seemed preposterous that a father would send his mistress to live with his sons, or maybe it was the thought that his sons would condone such a disrespect to their mother. So unbelievable that the very thought made him suddenly sure Mel was the mistress of the remaining brother, Luc. So the father's habits had been passed down through his progeny...

How many unclaimed children were there? Did Christian have more siblings walking around Chicago? The thought was a comfort in the way that the unhappy enjoy the pain of others. As shameful as it was, it made him feel less alone. He only wished he'd known them. Who knows, they might have formed a sort of private school, all of them unable to bear attending public school with the children who mocked them for their fatherlessness. The idea of another generation being born, perhaps from not one man but now his three sons, made Christian sick. He pushed off the fence and went to his horse, Blue. A mount of the finest breeding. He almost laughed as he stroked

Blue's nose. He'd never thought about it before, but perhaps his need to own such a fine mount was about exactly that. Breeding.

The clip clop of hooves alerted him to another person in the stables. An auburn-haired woman rode in on a mount as fine as Blue. She smiled at him as she slid down and led the horse near his own.

"You must be Willem's guest." She stretched out her hand. "Ivete Graham."

It was an effort to stay on his feet. He took her hand and prayed he wouldn't blush. She was a beauty, and he had to remind himself they shared blood. "Christian Milnes."

She jerked her head toward the entrance. "My husband and I have a farm farther along in the valley." She reached up and stroked Blue's mane. "Please tell me Bastien has purchased this beast."

Christian let out a nervous laugh. "No, this is mine."

She lifted a brow. "Ever thought of breeding him?"

"I'm afraid he's a gelding."

Ivete nodded as though she'd expected as much. "Is he from Carnege's stables?"

Now *this* was a horsewoman. Christian nodded with appreciation. "Yes." Had she been to Carnege's? His mind whirled with the possibilities. He might have seen her before now.

Ivete stroked Blue's nose and looked into one of the beast's dark eyes. "You might be too closely related to my stock to breed anyway." Ivete turned to Christian. "Are you headed out or in?"

Christian hadn't actually thought about a ride. He'd only come to get away from the brothers inside. "Out, I guess."

Ivete walked her horse to a post and began removing the halter and bit. "If you go south, there is a little pond that Bastien has made quite beautiful. I imagine Willem will take you if you stay a few days. But for now, it's a lovely ride around the water."

Christian, now committed, lifted his saddle from its stand and hefted it onto Blue. "I'll do just that. Thank you for the recommendation."

Before he'd finished saddling Blue, Willem joined him and saddled his own horse. The two men set off for the lake.

What had he been thinking coming here? Did he think just because he was as rich as his siblings, that he could now walk in their circles? He'd never have the breeding, the confidence. He was one of the racehorses that never got over shyness at the gate.

# 5

M el made sure the wind had dried her tears and prayed the cool air eased the puffiness around her eyes. She knew what she looked like after she cried. Her fair skin showed everything. No doubt Christian had known she'd been crying and made up that nonsense about a cat and mouse just to distract her. Her lips twitched at the thought.

Lydia caught her before she entered the house, Bridget on her hip and her other arm filled with tools. "Good morning. I was hoping to find you. Della said you wanted work, and I have just the job."

Mel gulped, afraid of what this woman would think when she learned Mel knew little about how to do anything of use. "Okay." She took the tools from Lydia's overfull arms.

Lydia ran her gaze down Mel's dress. "Do you have anything plainer?"

Mel shrugged. "Not really, but I'm not worried about ruining it. The chicken coop already got the better of me this morning."

Lydia lifted a brow. "The coop or the hens? They can be awfully greedy when they smell food."

"Both." Mel smiled and tried not to think of Christian who had somehow gotten the better of her in every encounter. He probably thought her a clumsy fool, hitting people with doors and snagging gowns in chicken wire.

Lydia gestured her along and they came to a large plot of dark earth. A white fence gated the entire section and both women stepped through a swinging gate.

Lydia set Bridget down, and the little girl promptly found a stick and dragged it along the fence as she walked.

Lydia pointed to a metal table. "Set the tools there." She put her hands on her hips and surveyed the garden. "On sunny days, we work in here." She pointed to the far end of the area. Small green plants grew in a long row. "Those are lettuce and the root vegetables are planted in the next three rows. They haven't come up yet. We need to turn the earth for row four and five and do a bit of planting if we can manage."

Lydia passed Mel a long apron that covered the length of her skirt. Turning dirt sounded easy enough. Mel tied the fabric around her waist and nodded as she looked at the wide plot of earth with new understanding. "Will we plant every one of these rows?"

Lydia laughed, "Not this week, but eventually this garden will be a sea of green, just you wait." She glanced at Mel's stomach. "You'll have the babe near harvest time." She nudged Mel with her elbow. "Be glad you'll miss the work that comes at the end. Planting isn't nearly as much work."

Mel tried to smile, but her lips wobbled. Her mother had died in childbirth. She'd much rather be harvesting vegetables than bearing a babe. She drew a deep breath that smelled of fecund earth. Her will was written down and Robert's last name added. Should she send it to someone? Who did she have to assure her will was carried out in the event of her death? Luc? No. She could not count on him. The only reason she was here with his family was because she carried one of his children. Would he even allow her wishes to be followed? Or would he ask one of these women to raise his child? Would he ask his own wife? Mel's throat went dry. Would they take her baby even if she weren't dead? If they did, would that be the worst thing? Perhaps she could forget this entire part of her life, live as though it had never happened. She placed a hand to her belly. Only, was it possible to forget one's own child?

Lydia handed Mel a trowel and glanced at Mel's palm pressed against her stomach. "There's no rush, we can do this work whenever. So if you're feeling sick or tired, take a break." Lydia knelt and stuck her trowel into the soft earth. "Luc didn't send you here to be a workhorse, but I know better than most what it feels like to live on another's charity and have no way to contribute."

Mel turned to Lydia, her interest piqued. "How long have you and Willem been married?"

"Six months is all. We haven't even started building a house of our own yet." She laughed, "I guess we're *still* living on the charity of family."

"A few months? But your children—"

"They're from my first marriage." Her face turned wistful. "But Willem isn't like most step-parents. He loves them like his own."

Mel turned the trowel over in her hands. Sure he did,

*now...* But what about when children of their own came? Everything would change once competition arrived.

Mel raised her gaze to find Lydia studying her. "If we each take a row," Lydia said, "we can work side by side."

Mel knelt in the row beside Lydia's, being sure her apron covered her skirt. After a few turns, Mel realized the work was laborious, but not difficult. The cool air and warm sun made the work almost pleasant.

Lydia cleared her throat. "Have you thought about what you'll do once the babe comes? I haven't heard any of the plans. Luc mostly tells Bastien everything, and by the time it gets to me, it's been watered down to nothing."

Mel stabbed her trowel into the earth. "I don't hear much either. I just go where he says. I don't have a choice in the matter."

Lydia straightened her back but kept her knees on the ground. "What do you mean? He isn't forcing you, is he?"

Mel shook her head and continued turning dirt so she didn't have to look at Lydia as she spoke. "I have no one else." She heaved a sigh. "I guess I should call myself lucky that it was him and not another man who..." She gulped, too humiliated to speak the words. She dared not look at Lydia, afraid the woman's face would hold disgust.

Lydia went back to work. "I heard many women had set their sights on Luc. I'm just surprised anyone was willing to cross Angelica."

Angelica. The name had rarely been spoken, and when it was it always held reverence. But Lydia seemed to speak it with fear. Or was it loathing?

Unwilling to allow any misunderstanding, Mel sat back on her heels and brushed dirt from her hands. "I didn't know he was married. I didn't have my sights set on him. I didn't even know his name before I met him. He had business with my uncle and visited us at their country estate. I've never even been to Chicago, not until I boarded the train for here."

Lydia squinted at Mel. "If your uncle knew Luc, he would have known to keep you far away from him."

Mel grit her teeth. "I think my uncle knew everything."

The two women stared at one another, and Mel waited for Lydia to understand, watched for any sign of doubt or disbelief.

Lydia jammed her trowel into the dirt. "That dirty pirate."

Mel laughed, but her laugh turned into a cry. She wasn't even sure if Lydia meant Luc, or Mel's uncle, but her indignation should have made Mel glad. Instead, tears fell down her cheeks.

Lydia reached a hand toward Mel. "Oh, honey."

Mel lifted her hands to cover her face. "They wanted me gone. I was a burden to them. I never expected this would be the way they planned it."

"Did they plan it with Luc?"

Mel sniffed and wiped her face, no doubt smudging it with dirt as well. "I don't think so, I think my uncle just turned a blind eye to Luc's pursuit."

"And I know plenty how Luc can be convincing. I'm glad you're here with us. I know we're Luc's family, but with you here, the women outnumber the men. We'll make sure you're treated fairly."

Mel dropped her hands and looked at Lydia. She wanted to believe her, but she thought of Della's coldness toward her. "I'm not sure all the women will agree with you."

Lydia drew a slow breath. "You're more right than you know. Ivete lives in the valley, and she and Angelica are childhood friends. Della is just cranky and ready to have that baby. If you think she hasn't been inviting, you'll have to find more courage to deal with Ivete. She's a firecracker and not well versed in looking at life from a perspective that isn't her own."

Mel's stomach turned and she covered her mouth, afraid she might retch.

Lydia cocked her head, a look of sympathy on her face. "That's good. I won't judge you if you use your condition to your advantage." She smirked.

Mel wanted to laugh, but the sick feeling, once acknowledged, grew, and she had to step outside the gate to empty her stomach into a patch of tall grass that grew along the fence. When she was done, she stumbled away from the mess and sat on the ground, leaning against the fence. Unlike a normal sickness, the feeling didn't ebb once she'd been sick. It lingered, a reminder of her mistakes. Nothing was as simple as she had once thought.

Family didn't care for others. They cared only for their own. When a man tells you he loves you, it is not because he does, it is because he wants you to believe him. She'd believed Luc so easily. He hardly had to try. She'd wanted to believe him. And now he'd put her here saying he would take care of her and the baby. But what was the truth? Did he send her here so she would work and lose the baby? Did he want her to *have* the baby so he and his wife could raise it as their own? Did he plan to build her a home of her own where she would live? Would he visit as though they were his second family? Would she be expected to love him in the ways of a wife?

If she weren't so tired from being sick she might have kicked the ground in a rage at that sort of treatment. But rage was not a luxury she could afford. Good behavior was her only currency and had been for some time. She would smile and be grateful for what she got. If she was lucky, that would be enough and she could stay in comfort. Her aunt and uncle hadn't been able to find another family to foist her upon. With a baby and a ruined reputation, she'd lost all hope of being saved. Luc—the Grahams—was her only option.

As she surveyed the scene before her, idyllic in its simplicity, a large horse and rider galloped into the frame. Christian. A youth met him at the mouth of the stables and took the reins. A few words were exchanged, but Mel was too far away to hear. Christian turned to her and started her way. She wiped at her face, wondering if she was still flushed from being sick. She didn't trust herself to stand, afraid the movement would make her ill once more.

"Ms. Williams. Why do I always find you leaning on fences?"

Mel laughed. "There is so much beauty to take in."

He kept his eyes on her. "Yes." He stepped closer to the fence, heading right for the tall grasses she'd just ruined.

"No!" She called out, flinging herself at his feet.

His eyes widened as he reached down and squatted to her level.

"You can't..." She glanced at the spot hoping he couldn't see or smell it. "Come over here, the view is better from here."

His eyes were small and unconvinced, but he settled on her other side. They both sat in silence looking forward.

He cleared his throat. "The view would have been the same from over there."

Mel didn't answer, rather she was too tired to lie. She

eyed him, he was no gentleman. He might look as tall and debonair as every Graham man on this ranch, but he was too curt to be of the same class as Luc and his brothers.

"What brings you to Willem's ranch? Why did you not wait for the usual group?"

Christian shrugged. "I was curious and didn't want to wait."

So he was impatient too. Most certainly not a gentleman. Gentlemen had honed all the virtuous qualities. Or that's what her tutors would have her believe was expected of gentle men and women.

Luc had used his education to perfect his words, to spin lies she still couldn't untangle. Had he *ever* loved her? He'd spoken of her need to prove her love to him, of how a man can prove it with gifts and words, but women had but one way to prove their fidelity to a man. Surely he hadn't spent all that time courting her just for one night, for that was all she'd given him. But one night had been enough to prove him right. She'd proven to him that she belonged to him. With that one night, she was now his to control, to move from ranch to ranch if he so chose.

Complete fidelity.

Perhaps *gentlemen* were exactly what Mel should avoid in future. But what future did she have without Luc? A fallen woman and her illegitimate child could not make a life for themselves.

Christian shifted in the grass. "What brings you here?"

She surveyed him. Did he truly know nothing? She didn't *look* pregnant, but it hadn't occurred to her that this man was ignorant to her plight. Apparently the Grahams were keeping her condition a secret.

She studied his features, the way his dark eyes seemed to look through her. She didn't want to lie. She was so sick of lies and deceit. But she shouldn't go against what the Grahams wanted, not when they were feeding and sheltering her. Omission would have to do.

"I am an orphan. I've been passed around since childhood, and I suppose I'll continue to be foisted upon others until I find a home of my own." She looked away, hardly caring if the Grahams decided to tell him exactly who she was and why she was here. What was the point in keeping the secret anyway? The truth of her words hit her like a bucket of cold water. She'd thought herself so grown. Being courted by a rich and handsome man. Yet that very man was treating her the same as any other man ever had. She eyed Christian. "Do you have a sister?"

Christian snorted, "No, thank the heavens."

Mel scanned the countryside beyond Christian. "I wonder if a man ever *wants* a daughter. We seem to be quite a nuisance."

Christian shook his head. "It's not that ... my mother is gone too."

Her gaze snapped back to him. His face showed no signs of sadness, her death must have happened long ago. "And your father?"

"Gone. Both of them are gone."

"Two orphans on a family ranch." She breathed a laugh. "Aren't we a pair?"

Willem stepped from the stables, tucking a pair of gloves into his pocket. "Ah, Christian, my good man. Bastien has just told me about a bit of property for sale. Care to ride out and look at it with me?"

Mel smirked at the man beside her. It didn't make sense men would come all this way just to be put to work. Nevertheless, Christian pressed to standing. When Mel made to stand, he reached a hand out to her. She took it, noticing his clean fingernails and calloused palm. He might not be a gentleman, but he wasn't a laborer either. He released her as soon as she was up, and with a nod he followed Willem along the garden fence. His frame, even his stride was familiar, as though they'd met in another life. Her tutor would have rapped her knuckles to hear such blasphemy. There was but one life to live, and so far, Mel had spent the entirety of hers pleasing others.

## 6
———

Just as Christian and Willem rounded the corner and out of sight, the front door to the farmhouse slammed shut, and an auburn-haired woman stomped over to Mel.

"You're Meliora?"

Mel gulped and nodded, rubbing her arms. She'd sat too long in the shade, and all the warmth from working in the garden had drained from her.

"I'm Ivete. Luc's sister and Angelica's best friend."

Mel's legs turned to jelly, but she stayed upright.

"I hate what you and Luc have done to her. She knows more than anyone realizes, but I dare not ask if she knows this." She ran her gaze down Mel's frame. "How many months?"

"A bit over two." Mel's voice was small, as though her mouth had forgotten how to speak.

Ivete breathed through her nose like an angry bull, ready to gorge a trespasser.

"The babe will come in October, then?"

Mel blinked her surprise at how quickly this woman did the math. She nodded.

"And what will you do when the babe comes?"

"I ... I don't know. Luc and I haven't discussed it."

Ivete looked like she would spit. "No doubt he's holding his cards, waiting to see what move he will be forced to make." She placed her hands on her hips. "Will you give it to Angelica to raise as her own? Will you leave it here with us and sneak off into the night?"

Mel wished she could say she had a plan. "I will not *sneak* anywhere. I've never done so and will not start now. I cannot speak for Luc."

She hoped Ivete was fair enough to have given Luc this same scolding. He'd done as bad as Mel had done, worse even. Only he didn't hold the baby in his belly.

Ivete's face softened just slightly. "How old are you?"

"Nineteen."

She jerked her gaze to the ridge line to her left as though this news disturbed her. "Have your parents tossed you out?"

"My parents have passed, and yes, my aunt and uncle 'tossed me out' as you say, when they learned of my condition."

"And now you are here."

"And now I am here."

Lydia came through the gate and stood to Mel's right. Mel tried not to read into the show of solidarity, but she was grateful for the feeling that someone, for once, was on her side.

Ivete leveled Mel with a stare. "This is a working ranch. You'll see even the guests work. You'll be expected to carry your weight."

Lydia shuffled her feet. "Ivete." Her tone was a warning.

Ivete's gaze flicked to Lydia for a second before returning to Mel. She raised her eyebrows.

Mel gave a single nod. "I'll carry my weight."

Lydia brushed her fingertips to Mel's arm. "Not too much. Ivete doesn't realize what pregnancy feels like."

"I realize plenty." Ivete's eyes were blazing.

Mel's shoulders curled slightly toward her chest but it appeared Ivete's stare did nothing to intimidate Lydia.

"Do you?" Lydia took a challenging step closer to Ivete.

"You were the one who told me it was good to wait, until three months, right? Just in case?"

Mel listened to the cryptic conversation with rapt attention. Hoping for some key that would make sense of Ivete's words.

"Well," Ivete continued. "I guess two Graham babies will be born this fall.

Lydia gasped and rushed to Ivete, taking her hands. "Three months? You didn't have to wait with *us*. That three month rule is only for the rest of the world. Does Thomas know?"

Mel ignored the happy women and returned to her row in the garden. She stabbed and churned the earth. *Were* two Grahams being born in the fall? Would her baby be a Graham, or would he be a Williams? What about when she married? The baby would take its step-father's name when that time came.

She swept her eyes over the expansive garden. She was one of them, and yet she wasn't. The constant theme of her life. Living with family, yet not belonging to them. When things went awry, she was the first to go. Do well in your studies, but not too well. Be beautiful and a credit to your aunt and uncle, but not so pretty that your cousins admire you. Be silent and invisible but not drab and boring. Would she ever find a place of her own where she could be who she was? She huffed a laugh. She didn't even know who that was. Too much time spent trying to please others meant she'd never tried to please herself. Now she was a fallen woman who might very soon be expected to live as a mistress.

What would happen if Luc visited? Would he expect her to love him? Would she have a choice? She'd never been alone before. Always had a bed to sleep and food at the table. She knew some children did it—lived as orphans on the street. She'd always counted herself lucky, but now she wished she'd had that experience and knew just what it took to live on her own.

A cough came from behind her. She twisted, her knees sinking deeper into the dirt, to find Ivete standing, her arms crossed. Mel waited, wondering what this awful woman would say next.

Ivete's eye shifted away then back to Mel. "I'm sorry. I was a bit hard on you."

Mel waited. Had Lydia somehow forced Ivete to apologize?

Ivete came nearer and looked down at Mel. She hovered for a moment then squatted at eye-level, her skirts brushing the loose dirt beneath them. "I wish you weren't pregnant." She drew in a deep breath. "But you are. I don't know what Luc plans to do with you once the babe comes." She glanced at the house and back to Mel. "I'm going to ask Bastien as soon as I've finished speaking with you. Luc truly didn't tell you any of his plans?"

Mel swallowed. This wasn't the first time she wished

she'd demanded answers from Luc. "He told me he'd take care of everything. It wasn't until he'd left that my cousin told me he was married." Mel lifted a shoulder, an attempt to shake off the hurtful memory, the words that had ruined everything. "I thought he meant to marry me."

Ivete reached out a hand, placing her fingers on Mel's knee. "What he did was wrong. But what he's doing, what you're both doing, is worse."

Mel's face crumpled. "What am I supposed to do?"

Ivete huffed. "I wish I knew. For now, will you accept my apology? Come to dinner at my house tonight. You can meet Thomas. Maybe he'll know what to do."

Mel surveyed the woman before her. She held back nothing. There was no guile to her. She said what she thought, no matter if her words sliced or comforted. As much as the truth hurt, Mel was grateful to hear it spoken so easily.

She nodded. "I'll come."

Ivete sat back, a smile on her lips. "See you at six."

---

CHRISTIAN AND WILLEM were once again on horses riding through the valley. The air was chilly, but the sun had come through the clouds and warmed their backs.

Willem glanced over. "Are you a land-owner?"

Christian gave a rueful smile. "I guess I am, though I've not yet visited it. My aunt and uncle purchased it on my behalf."

"With your surprise inheritance?"

Christian tried to smile because he knew Willem was teasing, but the thought of the money didn't bring him any great joy. It only reminded him how he should be on his way, how he'd made a plan for his future. He just needed to step into the boots he'd bought and move forward.

Willem glanced at him. "What did you do before you got all that money?"

"I worked at a stable— Carnege's. Do you know it?"

"Know it? I was just there last time I was in the city." His gaze snaked around to Christian, sizing him up. "And what did you do there?"

"I was the veterinarian."

Willem's face stretched into a wide smile. "Well I'll be. Does Thomas know?"

Christian shook his head. "Haven't met him yet."

Willem looked forward again, but his smile remained. "Thomas has a mare pregnant with a set of twins. We can't find a veterinarian close enough to help with the birth." He gave Christian a stern look. "If you don't want to be pressed to stay a month, you may need to keep the details of your previous employment to yourself."

Many mares died birthing twins. It was unnatural for a horse to carry more than one. Likely one of the foals would be born dead, or die soon after.

A farmhouse came into view and the horses moved faster; no doubt they anticipated a break from the wind. A rider met them and stopped his horse near their own.

Willem turned to Christian, "This is Hugh Morris, he'll be showing us the parcel of land they intend to sell. Hugh, this is Christian Milnes, a guest at the ranch."

Hugh nodded. "Pleased to meet you."

Christian returned the nod and they set off. As Willem and Hugh spoke, it was apparent that although Hugh was more experienced, Willem was a quick learner. Christian admired how Willem was brave enough to take on anything no matter how little he knew about the subject. As he watched, any bitterness he felt began to melt. He stopped looking at Willem as someone who stole their father's affection, and rather realized he was just a man making his way in the world. Francis may not have raised or loved Christian like a father should, but he had provided him with the same inheritance, or so he said, as he had all his sons. Christian had as much chance to make something of himself as the legitimate Graham sons did.

Willem's voice made its way into Christian's thoughts. "Perhaps Christian could help look over any goats you want to sell and help us come to a fair price."

Christian nodded. "I'd be happy to."

Hugh led the way to the barn, and Willem rode next to Christian.

He leaned over and murmured, "Let's talk price at the house, not in front of Hugh."

Christian gave a slow nod. "I can't say much about price anyway, only the health of the animal."

Willem nodded as though that was all he wanted.

They made quick work of looking over the animals. A few of the goats had foot rot, but with Spring so near, it would clear up quickly.

Willem clapped Christian on the back. "I think a goat or two would be a fine addition. My guests could learn to make cheese and take a bit home when they go."

Christian smiled. Willem's mind was always working and applying everything to his ranch's success. He almost had a mind to book a week for himself.

As they rode for the main house Christian turned to Willem. "I heard you asking about Hugh's brother. What is it that ails him?"

"Malaria. It comes again and again. Treatment is expensive, and Lachlan is too weak to work much afterward. Bastien says the Morris's have needed to downsize their ranch for a time. Their boy, Otto, is set on leaving, so I guess now is the time."

"Malaria? Did he travel abroad?"

Willem shook his head. "Not as far as I know. And their pa was afflicted with Polio around twenty years ago."

Christian let out a low whistle. Some families had all the ill-luck.

Willem nodded. "Whichever one of us buys it will pay over value for the land and the goats. Hugh will come to the ranch and take Otto's place as a hand for Bastien. I think it will all work out."

Christian was touched at Bastien and Willem's willingness to help this family. They'd never experienced hardship, and yet they were aware of those who did and creative in their means of helping.

"Do you like fishing?" Willem asked.

Christian pulled a face, surprised at this sudden turn of topic. "Yes."

"My sister, Ivete, is excellent. She could take us out."

"Oh, I don't need to. I'm sure you've much to do with this option to buy from the Morris family."

Willem grinned. "I can think on it wherever we go. I want to make sure you get the full experience. We have clay pigeons and rifles if you're into sport shooting. Or Thomas might take you hunting if you can convince him to step away for a moment. In a few weeks we have a dance scheduled."

Christian laughed at the robust list. He wasn't here for the activities. "I won't be here that long. Probably set off tomorrow."

Willem smirked. "Unless Thomas convinces you to stay." He faced forward again. "Be mindful. There's much to fall in love with out here. If you're not careful, you might never go back."

Christian would never go *back*, never go home. He would go east instead. Yet ... coming so far west made him long to go farther. As far as the Pacific Ocean. To set his feet on the ground in a town where no one knew his parentage, or lack thereof. Where no one asked about his family. He had money now. He didn't have to go to North Carolina. He could set up his life wherever he chose. If he lived alone and stayed frugal, he might have enough to carry him to the end of his days on this earth. He could work when he wanted, caring for his neighbor's stock.

Willem cleared his throat. "Will anyone miss you while you're here?"

Christian sighed. "I've no wife. I left my post with Carnege before my departure."

Willem chuckled. "I still can't believe you're a veterinarian. When Bastien finds out, he's going to want to keep you."

Christian laughed. "Does he often collect people?"

Willem cocked his head thoughtfully. "Actually, I think he might. Every single person in this valley is here because of him. But what he'll be interested in is knowing we have a veterinarian in our midst. Mark my words, he'll have you checking over every animal on his and Thomas's land before you leave."

Christian shrugged. "I'd be glad to." He found the words were true. The thought of them needing him somehow countered his own desperate need to meet them. It would mean at least another day, maybe two, but there was no rush. He knew once he left, he would never return.

At the house, they reined in their horses and climbed down. Willem jerked his chin toward the house. "You better go give Bastien the news." He put out his hand, palm up, waiting for Christian to pass him the reins.

Christian smiled and dropped Blue's reins in Willem's hand. He would tell Bastien, check the stock and be on his way. He had no true need to learn the ins and outs of this ranch. He'd met Ivete and seen Luc from afar at a gaming club. Unless he intended to search Chicago and the surrounding areas for other half-siblings, he ought to make his way east. Or west. The direction didn't matter. Only that he go.

———

CHRISTIAN WAS in the stables looking over Bastien's livestock when Ivete approached him. She wore a brimmed hat with fishing flies lined along the band. "How much more do you have here? Willem is afraid you'll work too hard. How about a trip down to the lake? I have a bit of fishing to do before dinner."

Christian looked around the stables. He'd not finished, but something about this woman pulled him to her. It was different from Mel's pull; hers came from a brokenness that both disturbed and called to him. Perhaps Ivete was different because it was the call of blood. He'd never known a sibling, so who was he to speculate?

He removed his gloves and tucked them into his back pocket. "I can finish the rest later."

Ivete smiled. "Or tomorrow. There's no rush." She

jerked her head down the aisle. "Saddle your horse. I'll find you a pole."

He obeyed, shutting the stall door behind him with a resounding click. He'd never pictured a sister like her. With her thick braid down her back, she looked like she belonged in some rustic cabin in remote mountains, yet he knew she'd grown up in the Graham mansion. He shook his head. He should stop thinking of her as a sister, for she was hardly that. She would never think of him as a brother, not even if she knew his parentage. He'd rather keep that to himself and not experience what kind of hurt the truth would bring.

# 7

Ivete led Christian to a rocky delta.

Right away he saw several pools where he'd like to drop a line. He glanced at Ivete. "This is a great spot."

She flashed him a smile. "The view is prettiest over there, but the fish don't seem to care."

He followed her finger and saw an area where the brush had been cleared for a beach. He wouldn't mind a picnic, or even a nap, on that beach. But no, he wasn't staying for picnics. He didn't even have to stay to finish tending the animals.

But he wanted to help. He'd only just met everyone, and if they needed him, he'd stay to finish the job.

Ivete gestured him over and pointed to a hole. "Are you familiar with fly fishing?"

He nodded and accepted a leather fold of hand-tied flies. "I'm surprised you are. I grew up in the country. Are there many rivers in the city?"

Ivete laughed and shook her head. "I spent time on my grandparents' estate. Near you, actually. Willem said you're from Aurora?"

Christian kept his head down as he focused on tying the fly, but his stomach clenched. He didn't want to lie, but fear of the truth twisted in his belly. "Yes." He kept his eyes away from hers, afraid she would learn everything with just a look. He pulled some string from the reel and waved his rod, sending the light line and fly soaring through the air. Back and forth. His movements were jerky, and the end popped. He drew a slow breath to calm his nerves and focused on the sway of his arm and, by extension, the rod. The motion allowed him a reason to keep his eyes away from Ivete's inquisition.

Ivete walked farther up the creek and cast her line. They faced away from one another, and Christian breathed a sigh of relief. They fished in silence, each of them pulling a few fish from the water and lining them up along the shore. Christian cast again, determined to catch a bigger one, but he smiled, not truly minding if Ivete bested him in this. What would it have been like to be raised side-by-side with these siblings? What if his mother had abandoned him to the Grahams? Surely, his adoptive mother would have hated him, but what of his siblings? He looked like them, to be sure.

Perhaps it would have been better all around. His own mother could have forgotten him, could have married and lived an easier life. One without shame or embarrassment. She would not have had to protect her son from bullies. And what of her? Surely she experienced the same treatment as he. Humans didn't turn nice when they grew to adulthood. He'd been terribly disappointed to learn they remained much the same. When she'd pulled him from school to be privately tutored, he'd thought it was because they needed to get through the difficult years, that once school was over, he would be able to mingle with people as an adult.

Not true. Instead, he'd left for schooling and learned to be a veterinarian. He'd worked at one of the most prestigious breeding stables in America. And still he pretended his father was dead. Still he would not admit his worthlessness to one of two people who should have loved him most.

He waded a bit deeper and cast again. When he got to North Carolina, he would marry. He would find a wife with a family background that would please the inquiries of their friends. If anyone asked about his parents, he would mention his mother and when the time came to speak of his father he would divert the questioning to his wife and her parents. He nodded. It was a good plan.

He began reeling in his line to cast it once more when the horses started whinnying and pulling against their tethers. He glanced around, trying to locate what was making them so skittish. Nothing. He set his pole on the pebbly shore and jogged over to the mounts. Just as he reached them, Ivete's mare, eyes wide in fear, tugged hard enough that the rein unwrapped from the tree limb, and it galloped off toward home. Christian took Blue's bridle, holding it firm to his mount so the horse didn't follow its friend.

A shriek came from the lake. He spun.

A large brown bear had one huge paw on their pile of fish, its teeth ripping one apart. He gulped and saw Ivete watching the bear, too, frozen in place. Ivete had been fishing farther along the creek, and there was a steep hill to her right. Christian couldn't scare the bear, or else it might turn and run toward Ivete. But she couldn't get to him without stumbling up the steep hillside. Along that same hillside came a tiny bear cub. The air left Christian's lungs. A mother bear, likely starving from hibernating, and now a cub. He swallowed and raised a hand to tell Ivete to stay put. Then he put a finger to his lips to signal silence.

He climbed onto his horse and kicked it closer to Ivete and the bear. Blue walked slowly, but Christian kept the reins tight and the horse on the correct route. When he neared, he was able to see Ivete's eyes. They were huge, and her bottom lip trembled. Should he ride his horse for Ivete? Possibly it would scare the bear away, and if it attacked, it would get his mount first, giving him and Ivete a chance to get away. He drew a bolstering breath and shouted, kicking his horse forward. Blue tried to turn, but Christian kept the horse moving toward the bear.

The bear raised onto its hind legs and let out a deep growl. It held its ground, but Christian and his horse ran around it and stopped near Ivete. She jumped onto the horse and Christian turned Blue and kicked him up the hill. He glanced over his shoulder to see the bear follow them for a few steps until it reached its baby. Then it stopped, perhaps maternal instinct overcoming its anger at being disturbed.

They rode, Ivete holding on tight to his waist, until they found her mare eating grass nearer the house. Ivete climbed down and then back onto her own horse. Christian followed her to her house, and they tied their horses at the hitching post. Ivete jumped off and leaned forward, placing her hands above her knees and taking huge breaths.

Christian stepped closer to her, his hands hovering. He wanted to comfort her, but he was unsure how.

She cocked a brow up at him. "Thomas is never going to let me fish again."

Christian bobbed his head once to the side. He couldn't blame her husband if he forbade such an endeavor. If Ivete had been alone, she might be dead now. Or still stuck near the water, waiting for the bear to finish its meal or turn to her for more food to fill its belly.

"Did you see the cub?" Christian shook his head. "That could have been much worse."

Ivete straightened and walked to the barn "Thomas!"

Christian stayed where he was, unsure whether to leave or stay. He'd just mounted his horse when Ivete, and a man—Thomas, likely—exited the barn. Thomas surveyed him with a critical eye.

Ivete stepped forward. "Please, come to dinner, Christian. Meliora is coming too. I'd like to thank you for your gallant efforts today."

Christian scoffed. "I wasn't gallant. I'm sure I was as afraid as you."

Thomas stepped to his wife's side and wrapped an arm around her waist. "Still, we'd like to thank you."

Christian nodded. "What time?"

Ivete squinted at the sun. "I told Meliora six, so I better hustle to scrounge something up." She turned and left.

Christian gave Thomas a tight smile. "See you then." He turned his horse for the bunkhouse. As he rode, he smiled in awe of the brave woman who shared his blood.

---

MEL MET him in the stables just as Christian was giving Blue oats.

"Are you ready?"

She nodded and turned. He caught up to her with a few long strides and walked at her side. He remembered her words on why she was here, that she was a burden to the Grahams. Yes, a mistress would be a burden, and as he watched the women allow her into their homes and activities, he was puzzled. Perhaps she was a cousin of some sort, and they had allegiances to her separate from Luc.

"You said you are here because your family passes you around?"

She glanced at him with sharp eyes. "Yes." Her word was slow as though she wished not to answer.

"So, you are family to the Grahams?"

She chewed on her bottom lip then released it to draw a breath. "No."

He almost laughed. He'd expected her to lie. Her honesty sliced at his conscience, at his attempt to catch her in a lie. It shouldn't matter to him who she was, and he knew she wasn't family. She would tell him the truth if she wanted.

"Ivete is quite the fisherwoman," he said. "Have you ever been?"

"Fishing?" she glanced at him, then back at the path. "Yes. Nobody would call me a fisherwoman though."

Christian smiled. "You said you know many things but aren't capable at any of them. What are you good at?" He watched her, waiting for her to turn those green eyes on him. But she kept her face down and picked at her nails. "School."

Christian laughed. "School? But that's no fun. Did you go to university?"

She snorted, but it lacked the humor of laughter. "No. My aunt and uncle would never have spent the money."

Christian nodded. Fool comment. Why did he criticize

the one thing she'd admitted she was proficient in? "What subject did you like?"

The ground crunched beneath their feet as he waited for her reply.

"Mathematics."

Christian raised his brows. "So you like numbers? Have you ever thought to work in balancing ledgers?"

She looked at him with knit eyebrows, confusion plain on her face. "I've never worked."

Did she not *want* work? He almost gave a bitter laugh. Perhaps she intended to live the exact life his own mother had. A life of leisure paid for by the man who would never acknowledge her. "You worked today, with Lydia."

She shook her head. "That was chores. They don't count."

Christian laughed. "That might be a comment best kept to yourself. I imagine those women feel differently."

She scoffed. "I didn't mean it like that."

"Actually, they have a girl who comes from another household and she gets paid to do that type of *work*."

"Stop." Mel laughed as she sliced a hand through the air. "I misspoke. That *is* work, but I was raised in households where women do not contribute *financially*. They tend to tasks, but they have employees who do the harder jobs. I've never thought much about what type of work I would do for pay."

"Maybe you should." If she did, she might find herself with the option to live free from Luc. She wouldn't have to be his mistress just because she had been before.

They reached Ivete and Thomas's home, and Christian rapped on the door.

Thomas opened it and smiled. "Welcome." He

reached out and shook Mel's hand. "Thomas McMullin. Pleased to meet you."

"Mel Williams."

He took them through into the kitchen where Ivete was setting food on the table.

Ivete glanced at Christian over a dish. "It's not fresh, and you know why."

Thomas clapped him on the back. "I'm glad you were there. Bastien and I have both asked her not to go alone. Now, hopefully, she'll understand why we are so insistent."

Mel had shrunk against the wall as though she wanted to disappear.

Christian turned to Ivete. "Whatever you've sorted out smells lovely."

The group sat and said grace.

Thomas turned to Christian and pressed him with a look. "Ivete says you're a veterinarian for Carnege?"

Christian nodded. "Used to be. I purchased some land near my aunt's home in North Carolina. Thought I might try something like Willem has done here."

Thomas's brow twitched. "Why not continue with animal care? Surely they've enough beasts in Carolina to keep you busy."

Christian shrugged, hoping to come across as nonchalant. "I might, but I'd heard so much about Willem's ranch here, I thought I should take a look before I headed East."

Christian took a large bite, hoping a full mouth would stop the questioning. He didn't have a sound reason for being here, had no plans to start a ranch like this one. He should have left, but he knew it was a matter of time before someone asked him to look over Thomas and Ivete's stock. As he watched Ivete and Mel discuss the garden, part of him wanted to stay, to see these people accept Mel in a way his mother had never been accepted. They must have some understanding of why she was there, and their friendliness to her went against everything he'd been taught his entire life.

His mother had been expelled from her own family. He still didn't know the welcome he'd receive in North Carolina. The aunt was the sole sibling who kept in touch, but he had never met her. The idea of Francis's family receiving him and his mother in any capacity was too far-fetched a scenario for his imagination to comprehend. If these women expected any sort of philandering behavior of their spouses, they would not welcome Mel into their world. The fact that this fallen woman was sitting at this table meant Ivete didn't know who Mel was and what she carried, or it meant Thomas, Willem and Bastien were different sorts of men than Luc and Francis.

## 8

Mel smiled as Christian bade farewell to the McMullins. Ivete had been kind, but Mel doubted she would ever be endeared to the woman. With a long breath, she started for the Grahams' home. Her feet weighed heavy with each step, nothing like Christian's long strides and wide smile. She glanced at him then back to the path that led to the Grahams' home. Though they walked far apart, they each treaded one of the twin paths grooved into the road by wagon wheels.

There had been a time when her virtue had been so precious that walking between houses with a man would have never been allowed. She knew little about the man who strolled next to her. They'd shared a train from Chicago, and he tended to animals. Was it his profession that had everyone trusting him so quickly? Her cousin, Robert, told her animals could sense evil. Was that why Ivete and Thomas trusted her to walk home alone with Christian? Or was it that she was already so low they thought she no longer faced any risk?

She suppressed a sigh. It had been an age since someone looked out for her, virtue or otherwise. Why could her aunt and uncle not have allowed her to remain? She could have stayed in and allowed Hannah her dances and courting. Rich as she was, Hannah would be married off in no time at all. And yet, they'd taken such a dislike to Mel that they might have sent her to a workhouse if Mel hadn't agreed to Luc's plan and traveled west. Her arms prickled and she pulled her shawl tighter.

"Are you cold?" Christian stared at her as though she were something precious, something to protect.

Or perhaps she only wished he, or anyone, would look at her that way. "A little."

HE SHOOK his jacket off and crossed the grassy middle of the road to place it on her shoulders. It still held his warmth, and while her mind told her to protest his action, her body relaxed under the added weight and warmth.

"Thank you."

"That shawl ... do you not have anything warmer?"

"I do. Only, when we left it was not so cold. It's as though I can feel the sun leaving."

He smiled. "Shall we walk faster? Get there before the sun disappears completely?"

Mel shook her head. She didn't have the energy. "This will do." She pulled his jacket tighter so it closed in the front. It smelled of spice and hay and sweat, similar to the way Luc smelled when he nestled close to her.

Luc. She hated him, and yet, he'd been the only person to ever show her love. At least, she'd thought it was love. But now it felt the same as the love all her relatives had shown her. Love given out of responsibility, of duty.

It wasn't what she remembered from her parents. And it wasn't what she'd hoped for in a man. She wanted more than care. She wanted adoration. She wanted what Hannah's parents were—blind to her faults. She looked at her stomach. Still flat and concealing what was within. Soon her faults would be on display for all to see. Fay would know. Christian would know. Any stranger visiting would know. They would see her belly and the empty spot next to her where a husband should be.

She glanced at Christian.

He turned his head so that he caught her movement and met her eyes. "You said you never got good at fishing — or anything. Why not?"

MEL TURNED BACK and stared at the yellows and oranges of the setting sun. "I was raised an orphan." She stopped, unwilling to spill her childhood to this stranger.

After a moment Christian chuckled. "I know that. Such an occurrence doesn't have to stunt you from experiencing and enjoying new things."

Mel chewed on the inside of her cheek. She needed to answer him without telling him everything. "I lived with aunts and uncles. And always cousins. It's as though my father's relatives all got together after my father died and decided I should live with children my own age."

"It's not terrible logic, but your voice says otherwise. Tell me why it was wrong in practice."

She glanced at him, his face hanging down as he kicked larger rocks from his path. "If I was too good in school, the instructors would report it to my uncle—as praise—but he took it to mean the teacher was spending more time teaching me than his own daughter. After that I sat at a separate table, and the instructor taught Hannah. I absorbed the lessons from the periphery."

"That's awful."

Mel shrugged. "It really wasn't. The teacher felt bad. Never told my uncle anything more about me. Taught me when he could. But Hannah knew. She would tattle to her father if I got too much attention in class."

"Was there not another family you could go to?"

Robert. "There was one other. I went to them first, but their children were all older. The youngest was four years older than me. They thought he could use a playmate, but we were too old for playing prince and princess."

"What? You weren't playful enough?" His voice held an incredulity and a bitterness that warmed Mel as well as his jacket on her arms.

Mel drew a slow breath. She and Robert had been the best of friends. Losing her parents had matured her in such a way that their age difference felt nonexistent. "They feared he was beginning to fancy me as more than a friend, more than a cousin."

From the corner of her eye she saw Christian's attention snap to her. Her cheeks warmed the same way they had when her aunt had accused Mel of charming her son. She hadn't known what her aunt had meant, not really, but she had understood clearly the disgust in the woman's voice. What was worse, they had loved Mel's beauty. Her aunt had bought her dresses and parasols, the maids had curled her hair, and she had been introduced to guests as the poor orphan they'd taken in. They had only wanted to show off how charitable they were, to claim any success of Mel's as the fruits of their own labors. Even at a young age Mel knew she had to please. That she was there on their goodness. Then, the very thing she'd been adored for had caused her ejection from the household.

Christian's voice drew her from her memories. "So they sent you to live with Hannah's family."

"Eventually, yes." She glanced at him, surprised at his ability to remember Hannah's name when the story held no relevance for him in any way.

"And now you're here."

Her toe caught on the uneven earth and she stumbled before righting herself and glancing at him. What did he know? He knew she was a stranger to the Grahams before her arrival. She was staying in the main house, but that could mean guest or family. "I'm a distant relative." *At least I carry a relative.*

He nodded as though her answer hadn't mattered at all, as though he hadn't even asked a question.

But he hadn't asked a question, had he? He'd merely been stating the facts, closing the book on her story of moving from place to place.

The story wasn't over though. She wouldn't live in Della's house forever. Would Luc build her a house on this land? Would her next move be on foot across this prairie and into Dragonfly Creek, or would it be farther? Would she cry on a train once more?

Christian kicked a rock off the path and into the grassy side. "I think it's high time you learned what you love. Surely no one here will begrudge you a little play, a little success."

Playing. She hadn't played freely since Robert's house. She'd been prim and proper. A credit to her new guardians, but not so much so that she might draw any attention from the men who courted their Hannah. No trouble in the schoolroom, but not too quick at the subjects either.

"What do you say?" Christian smirked, and Mel couldn't help but return the expression. "This is a ranch meant for entertainment. They've put me to work all day, surely they won't fault me for taking their best gardener out for a day."

Mel laughed. She was terrible at gardening. She'd never touched a trowel before that first day with Lydia. No, they wouldn't miss her. But perhaps Ivete would resent her shirking.

They'd reached the homestead and Bastien and Della's stable stood high above the horizon line. "What if I help you tomorrow to look over the McMullins' stock?"

Christian gave her a quizzical look. "You want to tend animals?"

"I've never done so before, so it would be both a new, exciting experience and a contribution."

A slow smile spread across his lips, but he kept his brows lowered as though he thought she was playing a trick on him. "Agreed, but when we're done you must promise to take a day for yourself. To try all the things your awful aunt and uncle wouldn't have let you try. Or worse—wouldn't let you *enjoy*. Do we have a deal?" He stuck out his hand across the middle grass.

She took it, and they shook once. "Deal."

---

CHRISTIAN SLIPPED his jacket back on as he watched Mel enter the house. Then he turned and made for his own bed. He retraced his steps and recalled their conversation. He almost couldn't blame her for seeking a change with

Luc. Why had her guardians been so awful? He could understand the want to protect one's own, but as an orphan she should have been looked after like their own. After all, she shared their blood.

He quickened his pace up the steps to the bunkhouse and entered. The space was as cold as the outside, and he kept his jacket on as he built a small fire in the stove. She was in his mind as he stacked kindling, then larger logs. When the flames licked up the sides, he didn't feel that usual rush of success. Rather, he felt dark and angry. How dare someone drive such a woman to desperate measures. He wished his mother was alive. This time not for himself, but for Mel. His mother was always taking in wounded animals. Surely, she would take in a wounded girl so like herself. What would Mother have thought of raising another Graham child? If her lungs had stayed strong, he had no doubt she would've done so. The more he thought of it, the more surprised he was that she hadn't taken to adopting orphans. Perhaps Francis would have disapproved. He might have rescinded his funding altogether, claiming the orphans were hers from another man.

He hated how little he knew about their relationship. He knew Francis visited when Christian was away at school. He'd heard the servants talk of a "master" when Christian hadn't been in the house at that time. He'd known, but denied it, forgot it.

He blew a frustrated breath through his lips. Not really. He remembered it all, and he'd resented his mother for her part in his creation. Such an act took two. But now, listening to Mel speak, he saw how, though two were needed, sometimes one could hold more accountability than the other.

Mel had been mistreated, made to think less of

herself. He gave a hard laugh. If she'd spent her life trying not to be noticed, she was the opposite now. She would never live in obscurity, would always be shadowed by shame, but that shadow would offer no protection. The world was too nosy, too smart, to stay ignorant. They would see her money, her comfort, and know she was no widow. He'd always pitied himself; not once had he imagined life from his mother's perspective. Now he couldn't stop himself from imagining Mel's future. What had happened that lead to Mel creating a child with Luc? Would her babe grow up with the same pain that had colored Christian's entire life? Would Mel's baby be a boy or a girl?

The fire popped and crackled, and he stared at the flames for a moment, remembering.

Shaking off the past, he closed the door and lowered the handle for the flue. He stripped down to his drawers and climbed under the heavy quilts, tucking them under his chin and closing his eyes against the cold.

In the darkness all he saw was Mel, her small frame walking beside him, her mouth slightly lifted in a smile. Other images came, ones that pained him to imagine. Luc, foggy though his face might be, drawing a smile, buying her a ticket, sending her off to his family's farm. After their father had revealed his name, Christian had asked about the Graham family. Luc Graham was well known in the clubs, and locating his half-brother had been too easy. He'd not had time to second-guess his endeavor. Once he'd seen the man—tall and dark-haired, so much like himself—he hadn't been able to resist meeting the rest of the family. Foolish though it was, the impulse had gripped him like a vice, preventing him from seeing all else, like blinders on a horse's harness. He had only been able to see one way. No other path had existed.

## 9

Christian found Mel at breakfast and smiled. She wasn't wearing a lacy dress like the one that had snagged on the chicken house. He was surprised she owned anything so plain, but perhaps she had borrowed it from another.

"You're still intent on helping me today?" he asked. He wanted to check on Thomas's pregnant mare, but there was no rush to see any of the other creatures today. "I could collect you when I'm through and we can do anything else."

She lifted her chin slightly. "I'm sure. I want to help."

Bastien came inside, his face drawn with fatigue. "Morning." He nearly growled at the room.

Della leaned over the counter. "Was it a bear?"

Bastien nodded. "Likely the same one Ivete encountered." He glanced at Christian. "How would a vet rid the place of a curious bear?"

"Same as any other I suppose. With a rifle and a pack of dogs."

Bastien frowned. "It's coming around in the night. I wonder if we could even find it in the day."

Della pressed away from the counter. "You're not hunting a bear in the dark."

Bastien came around the corner and pulled his wife into his arms. "I'm not? Why, when I know you'll take care of me as well as you did the last time?"

She grinned and pushed him away. "Will everyone help?"

Bastien shrugged. "I suppose. I'll speak to the Morrises today. Perhaps Hugh and Lachlan will join too."

"There's much to speak with them about anyway." She gave her husband a loaded look, probably something to do with the land Willem might buy or the prospect of hiring another of their sons.

Bastien turned to Christian. "Is it too ironic for a veterinarian to help kill a bear?"

Christian laughed. "Not at all. I've tended livestock that have been mauled. Not many survive."

After breakfast, Mel and Christian set off once more for the McMullins' place. They each kept to their side of the path as they had done the night before. Mel wore a long coat that hung below her hips, much better than the shawl she'd worn yesterday. Christian nodded to himself, glad she'd worn something warmer because the temperature had dropped from yesterday and they'd be outside or in the stables while they worked.

Thomas met them in the barn and threw a curious glance toward Mel. Christian waited, wondering if she'd explain her presence, but she met his gaze and said nothing. She stayed quiet, a shadow to him as Thomas introduced them around the stables. These beasts were tended only by Thomas and Ivete and were superior to the ones in Bastien's stalls.

Christian placed a hand on the smooth surface of a stall door. "Ivete said you mean to breed for racing?"

Thomas lifted a shoulder. "Breeding, yes. For racing?" A small smile played on his lips. "If we can, that would be wonderful, but we've decent stock, and there's more who need a horse than need a racer."

Christian laughed. "Carnege would say differently. Selling race horses has been his livelihood. Everything else just comes. Everyone wants a Carnege."

"Perhaps we'll gain a similar name for ourselves." He lifted his brows. "You planning to stay on? We'd welcome a veterinarian."

Christian ran a hand along the horse's ear, unable to stop himself from checking if the beast disliked the touch. "I'm just here for a spell. Let's see your pregnant girl."

Thomas moved down the aisle and bade them follow. "If you decide to stay on, I'm sure we can find you a bit of work in town too. You'd be busy enough. The nearest animal doc is in Wilsonville, half a day's ride away. We could use someone closer."

"I'll keep it in mind."

Thomas stopped and leaned over the gate of a stall.

Christian did the same and saw the horse, her belly stretched wider than one would think possible. "When do you expect her due?"

Thomas widened his gaze and shook his head. "If she were carrying one? Two or three weeks. But since it's two, I've no idea."

Christian nodded. "Likely within the week."

Thomas smirked. "Good timing."

Christian glanced at Mel then met Thomas's gaze. "We can take it from here."

"I'll leave you to it." He eyed Mel once more before he left and Christian bit his lips to stop a laugh from escaping.

When Thomas was out of the barn, Christian turned to Mel. "He's not sure what to do with you."

Mel laughed, but then her face fell. "Most people aren't."

Unwilling to let her wallow, Christian jutted his chin at the bucket filled with brushes. "You brush and keep her calm."

Mel plucked a brush from the bucket and ran it along the horse's back and rump, working around Christian. When she was done she took a different brush and worked on the horse's mane. As she brushed, she spoke to the beast.

"You'll be a fine mama. But you may have overdone it. Perhaps just one babe next time. It's sure to be easier than two."

Christian chuckled at her soft murmuring. He didn't have the heart to tell Mel that this horse might not live to see another pregnancy. If she lived through the birth, Christian would suggest not breeding her again, a difficult task at such a ranch. Perhaps they could sell her to a smaller farm.

When Christian was through with the animal, he walked to the pump and filled a bucket with fresh water. He scrubbed his hands with a rough bar of soap and shook them dry. "What's next, ma'am?"

Mel glanced around and shrugged. "Let's keep doing this."

He leveled her with a look. "You want to keep

checking livestock?"

She nodded.

Christian agreed, and they walked back into the stable. He didn't mind the work, he chose this profession because of it, but he didn't expect her to feel the same way. Nonetheless she worked at his side, soothing the beasts with kind words while he ran his hands along their frames and checked from the tips of their ears to the nails in their metal shoes.

Christian had a horse's hoof between his knees, and was cutting the sole down. He glanced up to see Mel eyeing his work with curiosity. He set the foot down and tucked the hooked knife back into his belt.

She glanced at Christian. "Does it hurt?"

"No, it's basically a giant toenail."

She pinched her face and he let out a laugh that filled the barn.

"Do you want to try?"

She stepped backward, shaking her head.

Christian laughed and gestured her closer. "You don't have to carve, but it's rather satisfying to get the horse to lift its foot for you."

She froze, like a cornered deer, then something in her face relaxed. She nodded, stepping forward. Christian watched her, unsure whether she wanted to do this or if she was merely pleasing him.

Christian led the way around the horse's front to the other leg and placed a hand on the horse's shoulder. "First, you want to let them know you're here. This girl knows what to do so she shouldn't give you any trouble." The horse was gentle enough that, although Mel was with child, he wasn't concerned about the horse hurting her in any way.

Mel nodded, chewing on her lip, in concentration or fear, he wasn't sure.

He looked away from her mouth and cleared his throat. "Then you'll run your hand down the leg and when you get to the fetlock you'll squeeze."

The horse lifted its foot, showing Christian and Mel the bottom of its hoof. Christian let it down and brushed the dirt and hair from his hands. "And there it is."

Mel gulped and stepped closer. She reached out, still facing Christian.

He stepped away, clearing the area for her to perform the task. "You'll want to turn around."

She spun, so her back faced Christian and the head of the horse. She ran her hand down, like Christian showed her and when she got to the bottom the horse didn't move. Christian came around to see what she was doing wrong. He knelt on the hay-strewn ground and touched the area just below the fetlock. "Here. Any higher and she'll ignore you."

Mel slid her hand down and tugged on the foot. Still nothing.

Christian tried not to smile. He didn't remember learning this as a boy. It had been so long ago and he'd done it so many times since then.

"Are you squeezing it?"

Mel nodded and huffed, letting the leg go and straightening. "I can't do it."

Christian stepped closer, putting a hand on her back. "Don't give up." He ran a hand along the horse's leg and pinched below the fetlock. The horse lifted its hoof and Christian let it down again. He nodded to Mel. "Let me see your hand."

She dropped her hand in his upturned palm and he

did his best not to melt into the warmth of her hand or the smoothness of her fingers. With his other hand he encircled her wrist with his thumb and middle finger, just below the knobby wrist bone. Her bones felt so dainty and some carnal want to protect this woman nearly choked him. He coughed, refocusing his attention. "Imagine you're squeezing here." He squeezed, then moved his fingers up above that bone. "Not here."

She took her hand back and mirrored his action with her fingers. She eyed the horse's foot and stepped forward. She ran her hand down the horse's leg and Christian watched Mel's arm, wishing he could run his hands along the length of her.

The horse lifted its foot and Mel jerked backward, apparently unprepared for the weight of the horse's leg. The foot dropped, but Mel's smile was bright and wide. "I did it!" she said with a laugh. She turned to the horse and patted its neck. "Aren't you a good girl?"

Christian clasped his hands behind his back, telling himself to behave, to forget how it felt to hold her hand in his or to see that triumphant smile brighten her face.

A noise came from farther in the stable and Christian turned to find Ivete coming toward them with a tray of food. "Mel, I didn't know you knew animals." She set the tray on an empty saddle stand.

Christian walked over, his stomach growling at the prospect of food. Ivete leaned against the wall and smiled at the other woman.

Mel approached, quiet once more, the way she had been with Thomas. A warmth spread in Christian's chest at the thought that she opened up around him. Now she was the shadow version again, trying not to be noticed.

"It was me," Christian admitted. "I begged her to come

help keep the animals calm while I worked."

Ivete nodded slowly, but her lips were pinched in a way that told Christian she was not at all convinced.

Mel's mouth opened, and she covered it with her palm as she failed to stifle a yawn.

Ivete raised her brows. "You've overworked this woman." She reached for Mel, "Would you like to take a rest inside? Thomas is out, and it's much quieter than Della's home."

Mel glanced at Christian like she wanted his approval.

He kept his face blank. He wanted her to take the break for herself, to tell him she needed it and it didn't matter what he thought. She would have to grow stronger if she expected to live with the scorn of living as a mistress.

"I'm fine." Her voice was small as she stepped forward, took a sandwich from the tray and nibbled at its corner.

She lifted her chin, but her shoulders curled in slightly. She was clearly exhausted.

"I thought I might walk to the lake next." He watched her, wondering what it would take for her to tell him no. Perhaps he should suggest a walk around the property line.

Ivete scoffed. "The lake? Are you looking to get eaten? You can't go there."

Christian laughed. "Do you intend to let that bear own your lake from now on?"

Ivete took a sandwich and leaned against the wall. "No, but it was only yesterday. You can't go alone."

"Mel will accompany me."

Ivete narrowed her eyes, looking from one to the other. She pushed away from the wall. "If you two are going, I'm going too."

Mel's eyes snapped to Ivete. "Actually, that rest sounds wonderful." She turned to Christian. "You won't go alone, though?"

He nodded. "You two are right, and I can't argue with the both of you. I'll go see what work Willem needs done."

Ivete chuckled. "No doubt he'll find something for you to do. He's always after some project or another." She passed an apple to Mel then gestured toward the house. "C'mon. Let's have a rest."

As he watched the two women move toward Ivete's home, Christian rolled his shoulders. He didn't feel great having pushed her about the rest. But he'd done so with the horse and she'd felt a moment of accomplishment. Why did he feel the need to test her boundaries? Was it merely the similarity to his mother that had him hyperfocused on Mel? Or was it the idea of her being a lone mother with limited options? Whatever she'd done thus far in her life hadn't served her well. Something for that woman had to change, and quickly. If there was one thing he knew, it was that a baby came whether anyone was ready for it or not.

———

MEL FOLLOWED Ivete to the house, grateful for the offer and for having been saved from the long trek to the lake. She'd not yet been, but Lydia had told her it was best to ride the distance. Just now she could have gone to sleep and slept until morning. A walk to the lake sounded like a literal nightmare.

Ivete turned and looked at Mel. "How was working with Christian?"

Mel yawned again. "It was fine. I had the easy job."

"Does he usually work with a companion?"

Mel's sharp eyes met Ivete's at the insinuation. "I don't know." Her face burned with humiliation at what Ivete was implying.

Ivete faced the house again. "He worked at Carnege's, you know. He's quite a hand at horses. I wonder how long he'll work for us before he wants pay."

Mel didn't know who Carnege was or anything about paying someone to look over stock. She'd watched Christian trim hooves and clean cuts on the many animals the McMullins owned. She supposed it was something the owner usually paid for, but the way Christian hummed as he worked made her think he did it for joy instead of money.

Ivete pushed inside the house and held the door for Mel. "I'm always tired at this time of the day. Are you still sick?"

Mel shook her head. "Not at all today."

Ivete nodded. "Mine comes and goes too. Every time it goes I hope it won't return, but Lydia says that's a sign of a healthy babe, so I guess I don't mind."

Mel followed Ivete through one doorway and then another until they were in a bedroom. "You can rest here. It's empty until the babe comes. Thomas has already started on the bassinet."

Mel smiled, but her heart ached at the thought. Ivete's babe would be loved and welcomed. Who would build a bassinet for Mel's baby? Who truly wanted it? Luc wanted a baby of his own, but with his wife. Mel wanted a baby some day, but not this way. Ivete had said two Grahams would be born in the fall, but one was planned, wanted. Mel's was not.

She sat on the bed, suddenly weary enough that she

thought she might sleep until dawn. She glanced at Ivete. "Will you wake me?"

Ivete smiled. "If you want."

Mel nodded.

Ivete turned and left the room, closing the door behind her.

Mel heard the door across the hall close. Ivete had probably gone to her own bed. Mel curled onto her side on top of the patchwork quilt and stared at the perfect stitching. Perhaps quilting would be a skill she could develop. She smiled to think of Christian helping her try out *that* new experience. Why was he invested in her journey anyway? He had plenty to do, and could be spending his free time with the men on this ranch. They all seemed so similar. Perhaps with enough time they would become the best of friends.

Mel, on the other hand, would never fit in at this place, not completely. Women were so different from men. Men opened doors and walked through them at will. Women had to wait for one to be opened for them. Either way, once one was open, there was always more than one woman clamoring to go through. Mel wasn't the sort to push her way through. Sometimes she wondered if she even cared to try anymore. But it wasn't just her anymore. Soon she would have a child and the need to speak up and take what they needed would be required. She wouldn't let the world push her child around the way it had done to her.

---

MEL WOKE with a start in the darkened room. Once the fog of sleep fell away she realized where she was and that she'd slept through dinner. She staggered out of the room and found Ivete and Thomas sitting at the table with empty dishes around them.

"I'm so sorry." Mel touched her hair, afraid she must look a mess.

Ivete smiled. "Have a seat." She stood, gesturing to a chair on Thomas's other side while she set off for the kitchen. "I'll get you an empty plate."

Mel chewed her lip and sat by Thomas, afraid to look at him and read what he thought of her on his face.

He cleared his throat. "Ivete says you helped Christian with the animals today."

Mel glanced up and saw a sweet smile on his face. His words didn't hold the cunning tone she'd heard in Ivete's voice earlier. "I don't think he *needed* my help, but he seems intent on helping me experience new things."

Thomas's brows raised and Mel's face warmed. She knew what he must be thinking of a woman like her. Unmarried, pregnant, and cavorting with men.

Ivete set a plate and bowl in front of Mel and found her seat. She leaned over the table and leveled Mel with a stare. "What kind of experiences?"

The heat in her face burned hot. "Innocent ones." Her voice was hard, and she held Ivete's gaze.

They battled for the briefest moments before Ivete nodded and leaned back in her seat as though Mel had passed some sort of test. "He must like you."

The idea wasn't as preposterous as Ivete speaking the words. Did this woman want to play matchmaker with her brother's mistress? It was a crooked idea, and yet the way Ivete smiled, Mel had to wonder.

"I've not had many chances to find what I am good at. Christian has taken it as his personal mission to remedy that situation." She couldn't defend his reasons. She didn't understand them herself.

Thomas reached over and took Ivete's hand in his own, a silent gesture Mel couldn't decipher. "What other experiences are you looking for?" he asked.

"I'm not looking for anything. I'm only here to live until whatever comes next." She was glad Christian wasn't here so she might speak openly. "I've told you I don't know Luc's plan." As she spoke the words, she decided to write to him, to demand the answers to questions she'd not had the courage to ask in person. "I don't know what is next. I don't know whether I'll live through the birth. My mother died giving birth to my younger brother. Maybe I'll be the same." Her voice cracked and she looked down at the stew in front of her. At the slightly blackened biscuit on the side. Her throat burned with the ache to cry.

Ivete slid her hand across the table and left it there, a comfort if Mel wanted to take it. Mel picked up her spoon and stirred at the contents of the bowl. "I'm beginning to wonder if any man has intentions that are true."

Ivete took her hand back and Mel regretted her words. She couldn't be too open with these people. They were Luc's people. They loved *him*. She was merely a rut in the road. A snag in a wooded path. The branch tugging on their skirts until the knot untangled and the body was free again.

She pressed away from the table. "I should get back. Della will be wondering where I am."

Ivete smiled. "She knows you are here. Christian came by and I begged him to deliver the message to Della."

Mel nodded. Was she supposed to stay the night or walk home in the dark, alone?

Ivete gestured to Mel's dinner. "Eat up. We'll walk you home when it's time."

Mel had almost finished when there was a knock on the door. Thomas opened it to find Christian. Mel gulped the last of her food, grateful to remove herself from Ivete's critical eye. That woman was suspicious of Mel to no end, and Mel was tired of trying to see everything through Ivete's eyes.

She peeked a glance at Christian. Why had he come back for her? Did he have intentions that were more than friendly? Was Mel safe walking home alone with him? They'd done so last night, but that was before he'd displayed a mysterious interest in her. Now with Ivete's questions, everything felt tainted. As though he wanted more from her.

A laugh nearly tumbled from her lips. She had only to tell him of her condition, and he'd not want to help her find any hidden talents. He'd not mourn her loss of childhood or think her aunt and uncle so awful. He'd run away, probably leave the ranch altogether just to get away from her.

She stood and walked her dishes to the sink.

Ivete joined her with a tight mouth. "We'll still walk you home. We should not have let you two walk alone last night. I wasn't thinking."

Mel glanced at the woman. Her words held the weight of guilt, but guilt for what? For leaving a young woman alone with a bachelor? Or for leaving her brother's woman alone with the same? If Mel had been Ivete's sister or daughter, she would not have forgotten to consider the proprieties, the dangers. The admission was kind, but the omission was where the truth lay. Ivete was trying to care, but she simply did not.

# 10

Christian lingered at the doorway, waiting for Ivete and Thomas to head for home. Before Mel turned to go inside, he touched her elbow. "We've worked all day. What do you want to do tomorrow?"

Mel looked at him through narrowed eyes. "It is inappropriate for us to be spending time like that with one another."

Christian jerked his head back at her sudden change of heart. He resisted the urge to glare at Ivete's retreating form. He needed just one guess to know where this idea had come from. "We don't have to be alone. Let's stay in and bake with Fay. Or garden with Lydia. Or paint the walls of the bunkhouse with Willem."

She watched him, and he had the odd sensation that she saw deeper than a human should be able. "I'd like to try quilting."

Christian grimaced. "Quilting?"

She nodded. "You need not stay. This is my adventure. You have already found your talent."

He was being cast aside. He narrowed his eyes. "I've

never tried quilting. Perhaps I have more than one talent that needs discovering."

She lowered her lids, but a ghost of a smile appeared on her lips. "Tomorrow then." She spun and entered the house.

He scrubbed a hand over his face. Quilting. Who *wanted* to learn to quilt?

---

CHRISTIAN MADE no objections as he pulled a chair over to sit down with four women at a quilting frame, but he was too embarrassed to meet their eyes.

Lydia smirked at him. "Actually, Christian, we need you underneath to pass our needles back to us."

He gave her a confused look and scanned the other women, hoping they would tell him it was a tease.

Mel barely suppressed a smile, and with a glare at her, he slid off his seat and sat under the quilt. He lay on his back, his feet sticking out from under the frame. The first needle passed through and he took it and poked it back through the hole.

Lydia's voice came from above. "Not the same hole. Pass it through just here." He saw the head of the needle poke through slightly to the left of the original hole. She passed it through again, and he passed it back the correct way. The others all had needles waiting to be passed back, and he hurriedly did his job. It became a sort of game, and he could tell by the laughter coming from above that they were enjoying the challenge. Too soon they were done and each chair slid out.

Mel's face dipped below the frame. "Many hands make light work."

Christian crawled out and sat back on his heels. "So? Was it everything you hoped?"

She smirked. "It was rather fun, but I wish to learn the stitching together part, rather than tying.

With growing apprehension, he watched her smile. Hopefully she was joking, but he supposed what they'd done was only a small portion of what quilting was.

Lydia approached, her hands on her hips. "Mel, let's get lunch together, then we can look at the patterns I have in the guesthouse." She turned to Christian. "You go help my husband with something or other. We'll bring lunch when it's ready." She waved her hand at him as though he were a pesky fly and not the man who'd just spent nearly an hour helping quilt.

He walked toward the door and thought to turn back before he left.

Mel watched him, or rather, his boots. When he stopped, she met his gaze, and he gave her a small smile before rounding the corner and losing sight of her. She hadn't smiled back, but she had looked.

Was it possible she enjoyed him as he was beginning to enjoy her? He had first wanted to help her find a vocation, something to give her options in life. He'd never expected to enjoy her company. He longed for her eyes to rest on him or to catch a glimpse of the slightest lift to her mouth.

He walked the property and found Willem hitching a horse to the same wagon they'd used for hauling fence posts.

Willem's face brightened when he saw Christian. "Ho, there." He brushed his hands together and leaned against the wagon. "Lydia says you were going to help them quilt today."

Christian might have blushed at the tease, but Willem's lighthearted way soothed any embarrassment. "I was rather snagged into it." He eyed the wagon. "Please give me something else to do before it happens again."

Willem guffawed and jerked a thumb at the wagon. "Climb in. There's a boulder I want for the front of my house."

Christian hopped into the back and faced Willem, who climbed onto the bench and snapped the reins.

"Your house that isn't built?" Christian asked.

Willem laughed. "Go easy on a man."

"How far along is the building? Where is it?" There was a cabin near Ivete's home, but that one was finished and vacant.

"Not far. I expect to get more done now that the snow has stopped." Willem pointed to the south ridge. "It'll be just along there."

Christian pictured a house up on the hill. The view would be incredible, but the road would be treacherous in the winter.

Willem continued. "We can't stay in Bastien's guesthouse forever. When I built the bunkhouse I didn't intend to have a wife to care for. Now we need a place for my family to live that is close to the bunkhouse."

Christian hadn't realized that Milo and Bridget weren't his, but the bunkhouse was less than a year old and both of those children were far beyond that. "How was that? Marrying into a family?"

Perhaps that's what Christian would do when he settled in North Carolina. Find a family who needed him and treat them how he'd always wanted. His mother had taught him well how to be a gentleman, how to treat a lady. He supposed there were others, like her, who needed a man that understood the struggle of a lone woman.

Willem laughed. "I didn't plan it. Still don't feel old enough to have a nine-year-old watching my every move."

Christian watched the back of Willem's head, surprised that he would settle for a widow with children when he could have chosen from several younger girls who had no grief or fatherless children. "It must not be too bad."

Willem cast a glance over his shoulder. "It's not bad in the least. You thinking of settling down?"

Christian drew a long breath. Ever since his mother died he'd thought of little else, not marriage exactly, but family. He hoped moving near his aunt and her family would cure that ache inside, the need for a family's love. Had he hoped to find it here? He almost laughed. They'd never love him because he was a representation of the very worst in their father. If they ever found out who he was they not only wouldn't love him, they'd hate him.

"Thought about it," Christian said. "I'm not sure I'm ready just yet. Maybe I'll find myself a nice girl when I get to North Carolina."

Willem smirked. "If you plan to start up a ranch like mine, you better find one who's scrappy." He gave a rueful shake of his head. "Some days I wonder that Lydia chose me. My mother offered to find her a nice man in the city."

Willem reined in the horses and both men stared at the large boulder that would need to be loaded into the wagon.

Christian looked sidelong at Willem. "You couldn't have loaded this by yourself."

Willem's smile widened. "No. I was waiting for you to be done with your needlework."

Christian chuckled and walked to the massive rock. "Can the horses pull this?"

Willem bounced his shoulders. "If you push, I'll pull." He pulled two long boards out of the wagon and set them up as a ramp leading from the ground to the wagon bed.

They both walked to the rock and rolled it to the wagon. Wrestling it up into the bed was much harder and by the time they were done each of them had bands of sweat around their hairlines.

Willem clapped Christian on the back. "I'm feeling a bit guilty. Why don't you lead the horses, and I'll push?"

Christian agreed, and they made the slow trek toward the house. When they'd gone halfway, Willem jogged up and took the reins.

He pointed to a small hill to their left. "We're going there."

Christian moved to the back to do his share of pushing, and he imagined a house on the small rise. The front grassy area would fill with wildflowers in a month or so. He looked at the valley, perfect in its natural way.

They unloaded the boulder and started the horses for home. Hugh was in the stable, and he took hold of the team, telling them Lydia had come looking for them not too long ago. They entered the house to find Mel working in Lydia's smaller kitchen with an ease he hadn't seen when she was with Ivete. He watched her move, wondering if the difference was that Lydia wasn't Luc's sister, or was it that Lydia had some other quality that Christian didn't see?

He glanced away and caught Willem's eye, one eyebrow raised. Willem glanced at Mel then back to Christian. Christian swallowed, wondering how much Willem thought he saw in that look. Lydia came and sat with them at the table, and Mel hovered in her usual way, sticking to the background and trying not to be seen.

Willem placed a hand on Lydia's lap. "We should play Codes tonight."

Lydia leaned slightly closer, smiling at him. They adored one another. Even someone like Christian, who had never been in love, could see it.

She nodded. "See if everyone else is up for it. Ivete might want to go to bed early."

Christian's brows twitched. Was Ivete ill in some way?

Lydia's gaze flicked to Mel then to Christian, her face red as if she were guilty of the words she'd spoken. What might have been an errant comment about Ivete being an early riser was now something more. Lydia's expression told him he wasn't supposed to hear it.

Willem leaned back in his chair. "I can convince them."

Lydia laughed. "I'm sure you can. But they may hate you come morning." She turned to Mel. "Are you up for a game after the children are in bed?"

Mel nodded, a smile on her face. Christian didn't yet know if it was genuine, but she hadn't unstuck herself from that wall since she'd helped serve lunch. He wanted to peel her off, to set her down at the table, or stand her right next to him, let her participate in the conversation with more than a gesture or a single word.

"Mel, did you often play games with your aunt, uncle, and cousin?"

Mel's placid face turned toward him. Her eyes tightened for a moment before widening to a pleasant, innocent size. "Not often."

Christian smirked at her vague answer. He'd doubted much fun was had with her wretched guardians. He smiled, pleased that she'd told him something she didn't want to share with everyone. And pleased at the flicker of a flame he saw when she almost glared at him.

When he looked at Willem again, the man was watching him with eyes that seemed to miss nothing. Christian dove into his meal so Willem couldn't read anything like guilt in his face. What did he have to be ashamed of? He wasn't doing anything but admiring the woman. Watching her was simply entertaining. After hearing about her childhood, he longed to heal the broken parts, to unlock the hidden parts, and to see her weightless.

His stomach sank. She would never be weightless. Not while she carried that baby in her belly, and less so after it was born. There were some things in life that time never healed.

He finished and stood, wiping his mouth with a napkin. "Shall we work on your house a bit more before supper?"

Willem nodded and stood. He kissed his wife on the mouth. Mel and Christian turned their faces away and caught one another's gaze. He almost laughed at Mel's scandalized expression. As though the thought of kissing a person was enough to make her die of embarrassment. But of course, she'd done that and more or she wouldn't have a baby in her belly. He clenched his teeth.

He hated that Luc was continuing the tradition of impregnating women and skirting them away out of sight. It would never end until someone stopped them. Yet who would force them? Not their wives. Not the children who had no idea who their father was until the second half of their life.

Willem touched Christian's arm, and he jerked away,

surveying the man. Willem likely had a woman some-where. Why would he not? How much easier it would be to live here and have a woman in Chicago. Such a big city, housing so many residents. The woman likely wouldn't even be known to the town like he and his mother had been. He glanced at Mel one last time before he followed Willem from the house.

Willem invited Christian to ride on the bench with him, and Christian had barely climbed up when Willem snapped the reins and the horses jerked forward. "You like her." His voice was level as though he didn't care either way.

Christian choked on his own spit and coughed, looking at Willem with watery eyes.

Willem stared forward, a satisfied expression on his face.

"I don't."

"You do." Willem glanced at Christian.

Christian couldn't help but clear his throat once more. He wanted to cough outright, but he feared the action would deem him a liar.

"I wonder if you knew her better if you would still look at her the way you do."

Christian picked at his nails. "How do I look at her?" Had *she* noticed? Had everyone?

"Like you want to scoop her up."

Christian laughed at the image. But the truth sobered him. "You think I should get to know her better before looking at her?"

Willem tilted his head but kept his eyes on the two horses in front of him. "I think you should stay away from her."

"Because she's pregnant?"

Willem jolted in his seat and stared at Christian with a wide-eyed expression. Christian couldn't help but lean back with a satisfied smile on his face.

Willem righted himself, and with a repentant twist of his mouth, he said, "I guess you know her well enough. I must say I'm shocked she told you."

"She didn't. I saw her on the train. Heard her and her friend saying goodbye." He thought of it again and gave a rueful laugh. "Fool coincidence that she ended up here." He raised both hands, palms up. "Then it all clicked into place."

"Does she know?"

Christian shook his head. "No." The thought sorrowed him. He could tell her he knew, but she had so little control, he didn't want to take any more from her. She could tell him if she wanted, and he hoped she would.

"Do you love her?"

Christian almost choked again. His half-brother had a way of rooting out everything Christian didn't know he felt. "No." Christian laughed. "No." Somehow saying it again only made it less true, so he clamped his lips tight.

"Will you tell her?"

There was nothing to tell. So he had *some* feelings for her. It was only that her situation was so close to his own. He wanted to protect her from his mother's fate. To stop the Grahams from taking everything they wanted and shouldering none of the consequences.

"My brother, Luc, is the father. He'll come, you know, and charm her. She'll forget she was ever angry with him."

Christian glared at his hands which were curled in his lap. He didn't doubt Willem's words. No doubt Francis had done the same to Christian's mother. Why would his sons not be equally versed in such deception? "He doesn't deserve her."

Willem shot Christian with a hard glare. "Deserving and having are different things, and I can tell you Luc doesn't know the difference. But who will stop him? Not her. She's too accommodating to go against his wishes."

Christian clenched his jaw, the discomfort in his teeth an anchor to his bitterness. Did Willem want him to stop Luc? Though Christian wanted exactly that, the idea that Willem wasn't faithful to his brother left an ache in his belly. Family was supposed to be more than words. More than shared blood. One should give everything for their family. Right?

Willem shifted in his seat. "I do not stand by his decision in this. I think you'll find I'm not the only sibling who shares that thought."

So they were all against Luc. And what did they feel for Mel? Did they want her gone? Did they want Luc to deal with his problems outside of their sphere? Out of sight, out of mind?

Willem stopped the wagon and climbed down. He unhitched the horses. The animals were also wet with sweat from hauling the boulder.

"Should I brush them down?" Christian asked.

Willem nodded. "If you would."

Christian removed the harness and bridle from the first horse, feeling that same lift of a weight carried, even though it wasn't his own. He brushed the beast down in silence, the work both calming his mind and allowing him to feel everything he'd suppressed. What did he want from Mel? He didn't want to leave her to her fate. But could he stay until she had the babe? Wait to see what fate she wanted?

Willem was right, if Luc had moved her here, it was because he intended to visit. And when he came what would Mel do? Would she go to him and thank him for the shelter he'd provided? Would she leave her baby with him and run away to find a life of her own? Neither thought brought Christian any joy.

It didn't matter though. She wasn't his concern. She would do whatever she wanted, and whatever he thought of that choice wouldn't sway her because he would never tell her.

# 11

Mel helped the women prepare for the game. The children were skirted off to bed early and each of the women, save Mel, produced a small treat to share. Even Ivete came from her house farther in the valley with a bowl covered with a cloth. Mel was grateful to finally have her appetite back, and she found herself ready for the game to begin so she might taste every one of these delicacies.

When the men came inside, the house felt full to the brim. Every man claimed his wife with a touch or even an arm wrapped around her waist. Mel thought of how Willem had kissed Lydia that morning. As though their love should not be hidden. She flushed again at the memory of how her and Christian's eyes had met. She'd wished she could disappear like a magician's bird. Now she sat across from Christian at the table, and as Willem explained the rules, she realized they were to be a pair for this game.

Willem added examples of how he and Lydia had bested everyone time after time. It was a wonder anyone else played at all, and Lydia's wry smile told Mel there was more that Willem did not reveal. The object of the game was to guess the code word. As the game progressed she realized she and Christian were at a disadvantage because they hardly knew one another. They had no chance of giving clues of familiarity. They could rely only on synonyms. Mel had always been a fool with words, and she bungled their every turn whether she was to give the clue or receive it. She watched Christian's face, searching for any hint of frustration. He would ask to switch teams. No doubt about it.

But he never did, and by the time it was over, she and he had not earned a single point. But who needed points when all the treats had ended up between them? Only Willem ate more than she and Christian.

Ivete gave a gaping yawn and stretched her arms. "You may have to carry me home." She smiled at Thomas. "Except I don't think my stomach could handle the pressure."

Lydia made a sympathetic face. "Are you still ill?" She glanced at Mel, then Christian, and back to Ivete.

"Yes. I wonder if it will ever stop." Ivete glanced at Christian. "You may as well know, since everyone else does. Thomas and I are expecting a little one in the fall." She set her hand to her stomach, smiling warmly at the announcement.

Mel's heart twisted at the joyful sight. Her chest felt like it was being crushed. That was the way a child should be announced to the world. Not in disappointment and disgrace.

Lydia sidled up to Mel and whispered. "And you? How have you been feeling?"

Mel forced herself to smile. "Today I've been well. I hope it's finally gone."

Lydia patted her arm and they stood side by side watching Ivete and Thomas leave. They were followed by Christian and shortly after Lydia and Willem left too.

Mel took the dishes from the table, tidying and readying to wash them in the sink. Della came over and placed a hand on Mel's arm. "Leave those for the morning. You must be exhausted."

Mel shrugged. "I'm not, actually." Perhaps the laughter and games had raised her spirits, no matter how poorly she played.

Della yawned. "Well, *I* am. Please, don't do too much. Fay can clean them in the morning. I'm headed to bed." She joined Bastien in the hall. Mel looked away, allowing them their privacy as they walked to their bedroom.

It was odd to live in such proximity. She'd never seen any of her aunts and uncles behave so openly affectionate. She assumed they acted lovingly behind closed doors, but there was never such an impression in the common areas. Mel smiled as she cleaned the dishes. Did her own future include such displays of love? Her smile slipped like a petal from a wilting rose. Her future. She had no idea what that looked like. But she might if she wrote the letter to Luc. She walked to the table and opened the sideboard, pulling out the ink and quill. All the lightness from the evening ebbed, leaving her with only sadness and anger. She sat, quill to paper.

*Luc,*

She lifted the quill and swallowed. What to say to him?

*I am well.*

True enough. But what else? She had no news of the

baby. She hadn't yet felt it move. It was no longer making her sick, but she'd never shared the fact that she'd been sick in the first place, so it seemed foolish to tell him it had stopped.

*Your family has treated me with unexpected kindness. I am anxious to know of your plans for our future—mine and the baby's. Will we be here until the baby is born? And after? I had not time to ask this of you when you told me you would sort everything out.*

Back then she'd been naive enough to believe that "sorting" meant a marriage license and a wedding.

*I beg answers from you now.*

She chewed her cheek trying to decide how to sign the end. She settled for nothing but her name, her last name written with double ink as though to remind him that she wasn't his, no matter that she wrote to beg him to reveal her future.

Her heart galloped in her chest as though it poured more anger into her limbs with every thump. She stood, glancing at the letter, the ink still wet and walked back to the sink and finished the dishes. When they were done, she still wasn't calm enough for bed. She went outside with only her wrap. She didn't need more. Her fury kept her warm. The icy wind of the spring evening hit her face, and each step soothed her until nothing remained within but emptiness.

How she hated being at the mercy of another. How she hated being a woman. Sometimes she hated even being alive. The cold air caused her nose to run, and she sniffed, wishing she had a kerchief. She sat on the bench that pressed up against the house. She could see the branches of a rose bush that would be beautiful come summer. Everything has its season. She sniffed again. Her season was short and wasted on a scheming uncle and a selfish man. She would never be young and free. Those adjectives were never meant to describe *her* life. Few women in this world were so lucky.

The shuffle of boots made her gasp and stand, wiping the wetness from her face.

"Mel?" Christian strode around the corner, his face a study in curiosity.

"Christian, what are you doing back here? I thought everyone had gone to bed."

"I came for a light." He held an unlit lantern aloft.

She nodded and led him inside. He followed her to the hearth in silence as though he didn't know the way. Once he'd lit his lantern, she followed him to the door intending to lock it behind him.

He stopped just before opening it and turned to her. "Thank you for being my partner tonight." He smiled. "Perhaps we should cheat next time."

Mel couldn't help but laugh. All the anger she'd felt for Luc had morphed into joy in Christian's presence. Christian was so honest, so good. The exact opposite of Luc. The thought of Christian cheating was laughable.

She gave him a sly look. "You cheat at games?"

He rolled his eyes to the ceiling and twisted his mouth. "Not usually, but I've never been so bad at one before."

Mel covered her next laugh. "I'm afraid that was me. I'm terrible at words. Always have been."

Christian nodded slowly. "That's right. You said numbers were your strength."

Mel nodded, touched at his remembering such an irrelevant subject.

Christian leaned against the door, abandoning any

pretense of leaving. "Can you apply numbers to quilting, or can we find you some other interest?"

Mel stuck out her chin. "Nobody is making you join me in my activities."

Christian grinned. "Oh, but if I stop now, I risk giving the impression I *wanted* to quilt. I cannot leave Aster Ridge with that as my legacy."

Her eyes flashed to him. "You're leaving?"

"Of course. I do not live here."

Mel's lighthearted attitude fled, and she couldn't fake a smile. She'd somehow fooled herself into believing he belonged here, that he was one of the men assigned to watch over her until Luc came to take her away.

"Of course." Mel swallowed, her throat thick. "I forgot you aren't a Graham." And neither was she. She glanced at his lit candle, the reason he'd returned. "Good night, Christian."

"Good night, Mel."

She shut the door and barred it, leaning against the wood. With a sigh she pressed herself away from it. She moved away from the entry where she'd pretended she was a young woman, flirting with a handsome man. For while those things were true, that was only the surface, like a mirror lake. She had yet to visit the body of water on the property, but she could imagine the view. Beautiful and fresh, yet underneath there were slimy creatures and algae-covered logs. One only had to look harder to find the ugly. So she would find that, in Christian. She would end this fantasy before it began.

She folded the letter she'd written to Luc and slid it into an envelope, writing his name on the outside. She took a spot of wax and melted it over the same fire that Christian had used to light his candle. When the wax was shimmering and runny, she walked it back over to her letter and poured it on the seal. She had no fancy press to make the wax into a beautiful shape. Instead she used the back of a spoon and smashed it into an ugly but useful splotch.

## 12

———

Christian walked his lit lantern back to the bunkhouse. Mel's words echoed in his mind. *I forgot you aren't a Graham.* Had he forgotten too? Had he begun to think that just because everyone was kind and welcoming, he was going to be allowed permanent residency? They might let him stay as their in-house veterinarian, but he couldn't lie to them forever, nor would he want to. He'd already lived the first of his life in shame; he wasn't about to live the rest of it in hiding.

He pushed through the bunkhouse door and kicked off his boots. He set the lantern down and readied for bed. He recalled her face. She'd watched him as she'd closed the door, as though loath to let him out of her sight. Did she want him to stay? He gave a hard laugh. Like Willem said, as soon as Luc returned, she would forget any foolish notions.

Christian would be gone before then. He had no desire to watch Luc manipulate Mel, to watch her bend and scrape for him. He could already imagine it, the way she did what others asked and never made a fuss. She likely thought an easy attitude would earn her a place at the table.

If he didn't have a place here, she had even less. He may not be a Graham, but he had Graham blood. She could spend all day every day planting their food, even harvesting it when the time came, but it didn't mean she belonged. If Luc's wife ever visited, Mel would be pushed out. And if Angelica ever had a baby Luc would have no need for Mel. And if, heaven forbid, Mel lost the baby...

Christian lit the stove and waited for the fire to grow before shutting the door on the flames.

The way Mel spoke of her relatives revealed much about her. She'd lived life quietly so as not to disturb them. She'd likely been the same way with Luc. He had but to ask for her love, and she had not the gumption to reject him.

Would she ever find the nerve to demand something better? If not for herself, perhaps for her child? Or would she live her life wherever Luc put her, as Christian's mother had done?

He climbed into his bunk and stared at the bottom of the bed above him. He needed to go. If being here wasn't a good idea, sharing the space with Mel was torture. The last thing he needed was to watch his mother's life on repeat. It hurt too badly. He would leave in the morning and be done with this entire family.

He wasn't a Graham. He would go to North Carolina and live as a Milnes and forget these people existed.

RATHER THAN PACKING HIS THINGS, the morning found Christian on his horse in a line of men heading to the forest. They were equipped with rifles and bullets. They also had food and gear if the bear hunt lasted overnight.

Willem dropped back and rode next to Christian. "You thought at all about being a veterinarian in these parts?"

Christian shook his head. "Nah, I need to head out. My aunt is expecting me."

Willem bobbed his head. "And when will you be leaving?"

"When we're done with this bear, I suppose."

"Don't stay on our account. There's enough of us without you." Willem laughed, glancing down the line of men on horses. All the Graham brothers were there and Thomas. Plus Otto, Hugh and Lachlan from the Morris family.

"I heard Otto is going west?"

"Yeah, Thomas has a friend out there, married to Otto's sister." He cast a glance at the Morrises and leaned in closer, speaking with a low voice. "Their dad is crippled. The boys have put their lives on hold to keep the family in food and shelter. Can't say I blame Otto for finding a place of his own."

Christian shifted in the saddle. Here he'd been, bitter at the money given to him. How ungrateful he'd been to forget that money changes everything. For good or ill. "And he's got family there."

"It's funny, the pull to family," Willem added. "I always loved my siblings, but I would have never expected I'd move away from Chicago to live this close to them. This is nothing like it was in Chicago. We're closer in more than proximity."

Christian's shoulders itched to turn his horse around, to leave this place. The adventure of a bear hunt should not have stopped him from going.

"And what of the fair Meliora?"

Christian kept his eyes ahead. Fair indeed. "I believe her heart is spoken for."

Willem laughed, but it held none of his usual joy. It was hard, bitter. "Luc will take whatever he can. He is a man used to getting everything, yet he earns nothing."

Christian surveyed Willem. Could that same descriptor be used for himself as well? "And you?"

A slight smile curled. "I'll admit, I had all the same luxuries, privileges, but Luc has always had more ... just more."

"And you want to see it taken from him? You want to see *her* taken from him?" She was a mere pawn to these people.

A flash of hurt crossed Willem's face. "It's not for me. No one here would wish to see her put up as a mistress. For her sake, for Angelica's, even for ours. How could our women continue to live with her, to love her?"

"Yet they have no issue loving Luc?"

"I never said that. Luc is hard for everyone to love. He takes and takes and never gives anything."

The anger in Willem's voice was palpable and infectious. Christian wanted to hit something. To hurt Luc and Francis for the careless way they wasted their womens' youth, their lives. He too wanted to see Mel taken from Luc. He wanted to see her set up somewhere, independent from Luc with a trade to support herself.

"Does she have anywhere to go?" Christian knew the answer, but wondered if Willem had realized it himself.

"Lydia says she doesn't. She's an orphan, and her family won't accept her back, not after this."

"Why don't you all take care of her? Let her live on your charity instead of Luc's?"

"Luc's?" Willem shook his head. "She's already living on our charity. Luc has done nothing but send Bastien a letter followed shortly by his woman."

"I guarantee she thinks she's here only because of Luc's charity."

Willem fell silent. Thoughtful. "In a way she is. We would not have known her but for Luc."

"And if she refuses to be Luc's mistress any longer? Can she still stay?"

Willem's mouth moved, but he couldn't seem to find words.

"So you see, she cannot win. If she accepts him, she cannot live among your family. Yet, if she refuses him, she will still not be welcome. She is here for a spell, and she knows it."

"You know her as well as I, better I would guess." Willem narrowed his eyes into a hard, assessing look. "If you know her so well, why not take her to North Carolina with you?"

"She is not my kin, and that baby in her belly does not carry my blood." Once the words were spoken, he realized it *was* his blood, at least a small part of it.

"You believe that because Luc is our brother that we owe this woman some fealty? Shall Lydia and I give her our money to live out the rest of her days?"

"You might give her a roof on your land."

"And what of when Luc and Angelica visit? We tell Angelica 'do not to look over there, for there sleeps the mother of your husband's child'?"

Willem had the right of it. It would be awkward, but the wrong had already been done. There was naught to do but live with it.

Willem glared into the trees, no doubt wishing he'd

stayed ahead of Christian and not come to speak with him.

"I bet you're glad I'll be on my way soon," Christian said.

Willem glanced at Christian, his brows still lowered. "It's not that." He exhaled through his nose. "I understand what you mean, but I don't know the proper course of action. No matter the choice, someone is hurt."

They rode in silence with only the tamping of hooves on the soft dirt of the path.

Willem turned to Christian. "Lydia says Mel didn't know. That she thought Luc a bachelor."

Christian was doubtful. A likely story told to the family so she wouldn't be the villain.

They arrived at the lake, and when they reached the delta where Ivete and Christian had seen the bear, they spread out and moved through the forest, each of them scanning the ground for scat. This took Christian away from Willem, and he was glad for the reprieve. Only it didn't last long.

Soon Thomas found his way behind Christian. "Can I beg you to stay for the birth of the twin foals? I'd pay you. In cash or even the mare if you're wanting her. I can't breed her again, not if I don't have a veterinarian living on our land."

The forest opened up, and Thomas trotted up to Christian's side. "Willem's guests arrive on Monday, but I've an empty cabin where you can stay. Hardly lived in. A week isn't too long to wait, is it?"

It wasn't, really. Not if Christian weren't lying to everyone. Not if he weren't watching a woman start the life that had killed his mother. But perhaps living near the McMullins would be the right answer. Ivete and Thomas didn't go to the main house for every meal. Likely he wouldn't have to see Mel at all if he didn't want to. And he didn't. She was everything wrong with his trip. Rather than meeting his brothers and sister with thought only to see their faces and how they lived, he was constantly reminded of the wrong that had been done to his mother. A wrong done by *their* father, and that age-old jealousy couldn't help but rise up.

But Thomas wanted him to stay, and whether it was that Ivete was the man's wife, or that Christian had seen many mares die birthing twins, he wanted to stay, to help.

"I'll stay."

Thomas hit his saddle horn, a wide smile on his face. "And you'll take the mare?"

"I'll not take anything. Everyone has been kind enough to have me here. You've fed both me and my horse. A week's not long."

And it wasn't. He would be fine to stay just a bit longer. Nothing would happen in a week that hadn't happened already.

## 13

Mel walked through rows of planted seeds in the garden, watering as Lydia readied the next few rows for planting. Bridget played nearby. Nothing had come up from the seeds they had planted. Lydia said it would be a month or more before they saw anything. Still, Mel watered the rows with the heavy can, her shoes muddy enough to show how much work she'd done.

"Mama!" Milo's voice called out, followed shortly by his gangly frame as he swung around the post that held the gate's latch. "Auntie Della says for you to come."

Lydia rose slowly, wiping her hands on her apron with a serious look on her face. "Did she say it's time for the baby?"

Milo shook his head. "She didn't say anything. Just for me to get you."

"Tell her I'm coming." Milo dashed off, and Lydia turned to Mel. "It's early."

"Too early?" Mel spoke, but her voice was too quiet. She stood and walked to Lydia. "How early?"

Lydia shook her head and lifted Bridget from where

she played under the garden table. Lydia brushed dirt from Bridget's dress as she walked toward the main house.

Mel left the watering can and ran to catch up. "If it's too early, will the baby die? Will Della?"

Lydia winced at her words. They were harsh, but Mel had to know. Why had her own mother died? Why was the ability to create life so often tied to death?

"Della should be fine. The baby might even be born alive. When they're born too early, I think it's a matter of the baby being strong enough to live outside the belly. Only time will tell us that answer."

They burst through the front door and Lydia called out, "Della? Is it the baby?"

When they came around the corner they saw Della leaning back on the sofa, her feet up on the cushions, and her head resting on a stack of pillows. "I think it's coming. Will you help me time these pains?"

Lydia nodded and knelt at her friend's feet. Mel stepped backward, wishing she'd stayed in the garden with the plants and dirt where it didn't much matter if a seed died in the ground. She glanced at her shoes, then at the marks she and Lydia had made traipsing through the house with filthy boots. She walked gingerly to the front door and removed her boots. Then she took up the broom and cleaned up the mess she and Lydia had brought inside.

Della groaned and Mel couldn't help but watch as she gripped Lydia's hands and her face pulled tighter in pain. Bile rose up Mel's throat, and she stepped out the front door, gagging, but nothing came up. She wasn't sick. She was scared.

"Milo!" Lydia called from inside. Mel returned to find

Lydia speaking to Milo. "Go get Auntie Ivete. Tell her to go for the midwife."

Milo set off at a sprint, right past Mel. Lydia's eyes followed her son's exit then fell on Mel. "We need warm water. Get the fire in the stove going."

Mel nodded. She shoved two logs into the oven and waited for the flames to lick up the sides before she closed the door. Bridget cried and clung to her mother, no doubt feeling the fear and tension in the room. Heavens, Mel felt it so intensely it was a wonder the child hadn't started bawling before now.

Mel shifted from one foot to the other. "Shall I go for Fay?" It was Saturday, and Fay remained at home with her family.

"No. Let her be." Della fairly panted.

Lydia turned to Mel and nodded, mouthing the word. "Go."

Mel understood and set to putting her muddy boots back on. Once outside she drew in a sharp breath of fresh air. The coolness cleared her mind, and she took long strides toward the Morris's farm. She'd never been but everyone said it was the only other house in their valley. Sure enough, once she rounded a bend, she could see it in the distance. It wasn't close, but the path was well worn, and there was no chance she would get lost.

When she arrived, Fay answered the door with a smile. "Mel, what a wonderful surprise." Then, as if something on Mel's face registered with Fay, her smile fell. "What is it?"

An older woman, presumably Fay's mother, appeared behind Fay.

Mel gulped. "It's Della. They think the baby is coming."

Mrs. Morris's eyes widened. "'Tis a terrible time to have a babe. With all of the able men gone. Shall we go for the midwife?"

Mel shook her head. "Ivete has been sent." She hoped. Now she wondered if sending a young child to deliver such an important message was the correct thing to do. What if Milo bungled the message and Ivete never went for the midwife but stayed by her fire knitting socks?

"We'll gather a few things and come with you."

Mel nodded, and Fay gestured for her to come inside. The fire was blazing and the house too warm for Mel's liking. Fay and her mother clinked and thumped in the kitchen, gathering items Mel would know nothing about. Apparently a birth was nothing new to them. She stepped nearer the fire to see a pictograph that hung on the wall. It was a lovely couple, the woman undoubtedly Fay's elder sister.

"She's beautiful, isn't she?" came a man's voice.

Mel jumped back, her hand flying to her mouth. She turned to see a man sunk into the chair as though he were part of it. "I—I'm sorry. I didn't see you there."

He laughed. His round cheekbones lifted so his eyes squinted as he spoke. "I apologize. I didn't mean to frighten you."

Mel's hand moved to her chest where her heart hadn't yet realized she wasn't in danger. "You must be Mr. Morris."

He gave a single nod. "That I am. And who would you be?"

"I'm Mel Williams. A guest of the Grahams."

"Are they taking women guests now? That's even more interesting than the men coming out here to labor."

Mel smiled. "No, I'm a family friend."

"Ah." He narrowed one eye, and Mel had the feeling he was trying to solve a puzzle. "You're not married?"

"No, sir." She gulped, feeling like she was back in her uncle's study waiting to be accepted or rejected from their household.

"I've three fine sons. Two of marrying age, and the last is perhaps closer to your age, but he's not yet ready to wed."

"Yes. Hugh and Lachlan brought me here from Billings, and I've seen Otto at the ranch. I saw them all just this morning before they set off to hunt the bear."

He nodded. "The farther west you go, the more men who need a wife. Though I suppose it isn't want for women that makes my sons not marry. It's want for money."

Mel blushed. She'd been taught never to speak of money with a guest, and here was this man telling Mel his sons couldn't marry because they were too poor.

"Oh, Pa, you're a terrible matchmaker." Fay tugged on Mel's hand and the two left the house.

"Sorry." Fay placed her bundle over one shoulder and moved her hair out of the way. "He's been melancholy as of late. I think it's Otto leaving."

"He stays in that chair?"

Fay nodded, bending down to tug one of her stockings higher. "His legs don't work. He had polio just after I was born."

Mel shivered and pulled her jacket higher on her neck. Five children and no man to provide. "How did your ma manage?" She stopped herself from saying the words "without income" though Mr. Morris had already made it clear he didn't mind speaking of finances.

"My brothers. And she did washing and mending. My

sister Eloise went to work for the Grahams when Della had Violet. Now I work in her place." Fay sighed, defeated as though there was no end to their struggle.

"And Otto will be leaving soon too?"

Fay nodded. Mrs. Morris exited the house, and the three of them set off for the Grahams'. Mrs. Morris kept a quick pace and by the time they arrived, Mel was breathing hard. Fay was not. How could Mel's lungs be so weak? But it wasn't just her lungs. Her legs were pulsing in a way that told her a walk to and from the Morris's wasn't anything they'd like to do again.

Mrs. Morris waltzed right into the house, going to Lydia and asking numerous questions. Fay hauled two large pots from under the counter and set them both on the stove. She added one more log to the fire inside and took two more smaller pots from under the sink. One of these she passed to Mel. "Let's get to filling these with water."

Fay led the way to the pump and, one small pot at a time, they filled the larger pots and waited for the water to boil. Della's groans rang louder, and the hum of anxiety in the house grew. Violet woke from her nap, and Fay took both her and Bridget to Lydia's guest house. Milo was nowhere to be seen, and Mel couldn't say whether or not he'd returned from delivering the message to Ivete. She thought to ask Lydia, but as she approached, she didn't dare interrupt. Lydia was capable. If she didn't yet know, she had a running clock in her head that would tell her when it was time to ask.

Della panted, and a sheen of sweat glistened on her forehead from her effort. If Mel thought a walk to the Morris's was difficult, apparently giving birth would be much more so. She'd expected a certain amount of difficulty, but seeing it so near ... her hands shook. She clutched them together, but it wouldn't stop. Della took large gulps of air, and it was more than Mel could take. She turned on her heel and left, tugging her jacket off the wall on her way.

Once outside, she slipped into it and buttoned it. She'd meant to go to the guest house with Fay, but she didn't stop once there. Her legs, once weak, now seemed intent to correct their weakness. She took long strides through the prairie. The wind at her back propelled her forward. She let it push her along, as she always had. She'd never chosen her own direction, always being told, being pushed along the path of least resistance.

The ground was wet, and the dampness found its way between the buttons of her boots. Her socks were becoming damp, her toes stiffening. She walked in the direction of the lake. The cold wind might have cleared her mind, but she couldn't stop thinking of Della, laboring over her babe. Mel couldn't remember her mother's labor, but with the image of Della fresh in her mind, she could well imagine it, as though her mother labored on that sofa, not Della.

Had her mother had women surrounding her, helping her? Or had she only had the family doctor who tended Mel's cuts and fevers? She could recall his face, and she grimaced at the thought of him tending her mother's labor, of seeing her take her last breath. The fear was back again. Mel wasn't in fit condition to labor as Della was doing. Della and Fay often worked side by side. They were strong women who worked all day every day. Mel only napped and planted seeds. She quickened her pace. The wind shifted and now blew in her face, but she would not stop. She was determined to see the lake.

She pushed harder, her legs tingling again like something flicked up and down them. It felt good, as though she was punishing her body for being weak. Her mind pushed her along, and her legs had no choice but to follow. Was a mind so powerful it could command the body not to die, and the body would obey?

She crested the top of the hill, gasping for air. Small dots of black appeared in her vision, but she blinked them away. The lake was beautiful. It wasn't glassy like she'd imagined. The wind that buffeted her now caused the surface to ripple and run up on the shore. She began the descent from her hill, and finally she reached the pebbled shore. She squatted down and picked up a pale pebble. It was round, smoothed by waves and windy days like this.

Her body begged to sit, to lie down, but she knew if she did, she might not be able to get back up. At the west end of the lake stood a forest like the one behind her cousin Robert's home. A small stream ran through and poured into the lake. She walked toward it. She and Robert would play for hours in the trees. She curled her hand into a ball, feeling the past on her fingertips, the way their hands would be tacky from the sap after climbing trees.

Tears sprang to her eyes, and she dashed them away, not knowing where they came from. Her days with Robert had been some of the happiest. He was the only person in the world who she felt loved her without expecting anything in return. He hadn't loved her in the way his mother thought. She'd been a little sister to him. Could she go to him now? Would his wife allow her to stay with them? Or would she think like Robert's mother? Or worse, would she think the babe was Robert's?

Mel reached the creek that fed the lake and found a

few stepping stones to cross the water without getting her skirts wet. She walked farther into the forest until all she could smell was pine. She closed her eyes and let the smell take her back to her youth, to the days when she'd healed from the loss of her father. She opened her eyes again and brushed her fingers along the bark of the tree. Her heart was so heavy with that touch, she could no longer deny her body's need to sit down.

Pine needles covered the floor and would protect her dress from the worst of the mud. She sat down, leaning against the tree. The bark pulled her hair from its coif, but she didn't care. Nothing mattered. Good or bad, her life would go the way someone else planned. She looked up the length of the towering trees to where they met the gray sky. She closed her eyes again and calmed her breathing.

Her life would be acceptable, as it had always been. Her life hadn't been anything spectacular, but it was something. She'd always been cared for, fed, sheltered. She had no fear that would change. Yet, that thought made her heavier still. The thought of living her future in the same way she'd lived her past made her chest ache and her shoulders sag. She leaned farther into the tree, her eyes still closed, and allowed herself to fall asleep.

# 14

A s Christian and the rest of the men dipped into the valley, Bastien's home crept into view, a trail of smoke streaming from the chimney. Christian's heart thumped at the prospect of a warm fire. They'd ridden most of the day with no sign of the bear. There wasn't any use in camping out. The bear could have been anywhere. They'd try again tomorrow in a different direction. Or better, the bear would come to them, and they would be able to easily track and hunt it.

The Morris boys insisted on taking Christian's horse and brushing it down for him. He guessed the Grahams were paying them to do so. Had they also been paid to help on the hunt? He passed the reins to the strongest looking brother, Hugh, and made his way into the house. It was hotter inside than he expected, too hot. He shed his coat and gloves and breathed in the wet air that reminded him of one of those hot boxes where one would pour water on hot rocks and sit in the steam.

Voices came from farther in. "Let's get her to the bedroom."

Bastien held Della aloft, and Christian only glimpsed moving bodies before they disappeared down the hall.

Willem stood next to Christian. "It's time." He rolled his shoulders. "I know women do it, but I don't know how Bastien can handle it. I don't know if I will be able to at all."

Christian nodded. Willem, of course, hadn't been there for the birth of any of Lydia's children. Christian clapped him on the back. "I hope you get to experience it. At least you know your woman can do it."

Christian looked around. Lydia and Mrs. Morris were speaking, head-to-head.

Christian nudged Willem. "Where are Fay and Mel? And the children?"

Lydia turned, her ears sharp. "They're in the guest house. Bridget was making a fuss."

Willem gestured Christian along, and they headed toward the guest house. Inside, Milo fairly jumped on Willem, telling him how he'd been the runner all over the valley to gather everyone, except of course Fay and Mrs. Morris. The way he looked at Fay told Christian that Milo thought of that woman with more adoration than he ought to at his age.

Mel was nowhere to be seen. Christian came nearer Willem and Fay. She had so many questions about Della's progress that Willem just laughed and said, "I've got the little ones now. You go. Help the women, and tell us if it's a boy or a girl."

Fay grabbed her shawl and wrapped it around her shoulders. She was just about to go when Christian touched her arm. "Where is Mel?"

Fay shrugged. "Inside, I guess."

She left, and a cold wind howled outside. A storm was

brewing, and Mel wasn't accounted for. He turned to Willem. "Mel is missing. She's not inside."

"Are you sure? Women with child do tend to take naps. Maybe she's just sleeping."

Christian nodded, but the way his stomach turned told him otherwise. "I'll check."

Willem smirked as he nodded at Christian. Then he turned to little Violet and touched his nose to hers, "He's going to check."

Christian walked back to the main house and found Fay. "Is she in here?"

Fay looked around as though she'd forgotten about Mel. "I guess she isn't." Christian turned to Lydia. "Did Mel lie down for a bit?"

Lydia shook her head. "I don't think so. I'll go check her room."

Christian tapped his boot as he waited for Lydia to return. She shook her head, a solemn turn to her mouth. "Maybe she went to Ivete's?"

Fay bit her nail. "Ivete went for the midwife."

Christian didn't need to hear any more. He jogged from the house and to the stables. His horse had yet to be unsaddled, and with a nod to Hugh he climbed back on and set off to Ivete's house.

When he arrived, the place was dark and likely empty. Nevertheless, he pounded on the door and called for Mel. Nothing. He rode to the lake. For where else would she be? Once he reached the top of the hill he looked down in the bowl where the lake lay and sighed. She was nowhere in sight. The wind was so powerful it made his eyes water.

"Mel!" he called, but the wind blew in his face, sweeping his cry away. He kicked his horse down the hill toward the forest that lined the west side of the lake. The wind blew east, so if he went west and called again, the wind would carry his message. He led Blue along the shore, the horse's hooves crunching in the pebbled bank. The noise kept drawing his eye as though he would find her on the ground beneath him. And just when he shook his head at his foolishness he saw it. A small shoe mark in the muddy grass. And another. He climbed off his horse and tracked the footprints. As he moved closer to the forest, his stomach lurched. Was she fool enough to go into the forest when there was a bear to be hunted?

*Yes.* Not that she was a fool, but she knew nothing about animals, about being in the wilds. He felt sure of it. He tied his horse to the first tree and crossed the river into the deeper forest. There, on the bank, he saw another footprint. She was here.

"Mel!" he called again into the trees. A frightened crow took flight with an angry caw. He should have brought the rifle Bastien had loaned him. He had nothing, not even a knife, which was likely still in his saddle unless Hugh had removed it. His heart pounded as he stepped on the muted pine needles. "Mel!"

"Christian?" A voice sounded from almost underneath him. Her muddied boots stuck out, and as he came around the tree the rest of her appeared. She climbed to her feet, covering a gaping yawn.

"Mel, what are you doing out here?"

"I was just..." She looked around. "What time is it?"

"Were you asleep? There's a *bear* in these woods."

She looked over her shoulder, as though the moment she awoke the bear would amble into her sphere. "I didn't mean to fall asleep." She yawned again. "I guess I was tired."

Christian wanted to curse, to spit. She was tired so she

came a mile from the house to sleep against a tree. He closed his eyes and slowed his breathing. Then he turned and stomped back to his horse. He could hear the whisper of her skirts along the pine needles as she followed him, and when they reached Blue, Christian held the reins and waved Mel over. The wind was stronger outside the cover of trees, and it blew her hair from her pins.

"Up you go," he ordered.

She obeyed, not meeting his eyes. She kept her hands and eyes on the saddle horn. With her hair a mess and her shoulders slumped, she looked younger than he first thought. She claimed nineteen, but she could be seventeen.

He started for home. "What were you thinking? Everyone is bound to be worried about you by now."

"I'm sorry. I didn't mean to go so far, or stay so long."

"What if night had fallen? What if that bear had come back. That's the very place we saw the bear last time."

"I didn't know that."

"You knew there was a bear."

"That you men were hunting."

"Well, we didn't kill it. It's out there somewhere, so stay close to the house."

She didn't reply, and he regretted the harshness of his voice. If she had argued back, it would have been fine, but her submissivness changed the argument and left a bitter taste in his mouth.

"I'm glad you're unhurt," he said, gentling his voice. "Let's get you back to everyone."

Since he wasn't riding, it took far longer to get to the house. Hugh was still in the stables and took the reins for a second time. Hugh looked at Mel, watching her face for long enough that Christian knew he admired her beauty.

Who wouldn't? The wind had loosened her hair so tendrils curled around her face and neck. Her tousled appearance made Christian believe he knew her better somehow, that this was what she would look like on a lazy Sunday morning having just risen for breakfast.

She swung her leg off the other side, showing the men more of her petticoats than she ought. Rather than jump down, she stared at Christian with raised eyebrows. He stepped forward and lifted her down from the saddle. Christian felt Hugh's gaze on Mel as she climbed down from the mount.

He supposed a woman with Mel's beauty might still marry. If she wasn't in love with Luc, she could still find a man to be the father of her babe. Then he remembered Willem's words. Luc was capable of charming her. She must love him. She must want the life Christian's mother had lived.

Why they settled for such might never be in his under-standing. He watched as she gave a small smile to Hugh then turned to Christian. She didn't meet his eyes, and he followed her to the house.

As he predicted, their arrival brought a clamor of questions and thanking the Lord.

Fay set two bowls of barley stew on the table and nodded at Christian. He took Mel's elbow and led her to the table to sit.

The house was far too crowded. The midwife had arrived, and Ivete sat near the fire with rosy cheeks. Thomas sat next to her, rubbing warmth back into her hands. Christian couldn't help but smile. The rich socialite had been the one to ride all over the countryside on a stormy evening.

Lydia went to and from Bastien and Della's bedroom,

bringing a clean towel or a cup of water. Mrs. Morris and Fay worked in the kitchen, Mrs. Morris cleaning nooks and crannies that must not be part of the usual job of tidying up.

Mel rose from her seat. "Would you like me to get you another bowl?"

Christian looked down. He'd been mopping up the rest of his stew. He nodded. "Please."

She took his bowl and her own and joined Fay and Mrs. Morris in the kitchen. She gave her bowl to Fay and took his to the pot to dish another portion. She set it in front of him, and he murmured his thanks. The moment the bowl was out of her hands, she began wringing them together and glancing down the hall.

He finished chewing and said, "I was going to join Willem out in the guest house with the children. Would you like to come?"

She glanced at him as though he was interrupting her dire thoughts. "S-sure."

Christian took large bites and was finished with his second helping in less time than it took to eat his first. He stood and gave his bowl to Fay then notched his elbow, waiting to escort Mel outside.

She chewed her bottom lip, torn between staying and going. With a sigh, she conceded and took his arm. They stopped at the front, both of them slipping on their jackets. The walk to the guest house wasn't far, but the wind howled, and he knew it would be frightfully cold nonetheless.

They dashed from one house to the other, and when Christian shut the door behind them, Mel shuddered and clutched her coat tighter. Willem and Milo came around the corner with matching smiles on their faces. For all that they weren't father and son, Milo was his step-father's image in many ways.

Willem put a hand on Milo's head. "We're just getting the girls to bed."

Mel stepped forward as though she would help, but Willem put out a hand. "You find a seat by the fire. Violet is already asleep, and Milo is just going to finish reading Bridget her story. I'll be out soon."

With a nod, Mel turned and glanced at Christian before standing in front of the fire. She would hardly look at him. Was she that hurt by their conversation earlier? She held her hands out near the flames. Christian sat in a winged chair and longed to do the same. He still felt cold from riding in the icy wind all the day. The sound of it had stilled outside the house and in his ears. Perhaps the bear decided it was yet too cold to come out for the spring.

Mel sat down, her hands clasped tightly in her lap. Was it the cold that made her clutch them together, or was it the woman in the main house, giving birth as Mel would do in a few months?

"A babe." Christian tried to smile. "Won't that be nice?"

Mel kept her eyes down and nodded.

Christian cradled the back of his head. "I told Thomas I'd stay a week longer. He'd like help with the mare that's carrying twins."

Mel glanced at him then away. "A week." She shrugged. "Much longer than you planned. You've been here a week already."

"Have I overstayed my welcome then?" He watched her, a smile on his lips.

A small grin stretched her face. "Of course not. But ... this isn't my home to say so."

"And how long will you be staying?"

"A few months. I'm as aimless as you."

Christian chuckled. "I'm not aimless."

Mel looked at him with one eyebrow higher than the other. "No?"

Christian smiled, though her words stung. "I've a place in North Carolina. Family who is waiting for me to join them."

"You're not thrilled about it, else you would have been on your way long before now."

There was work to be done here. The Grahams needed his hands, and Thomas needed help with his mare's labor. But he couldn't say as much to Mel. He didn't want to say anything about a mother dying in birth to Mel, no matter that it was an animal.

"I don't know my aunt. Never met her in my life." He leaned forward, resting his elbows on his knees and clasping his hands. "I know not what will greet me when I arrive."

Mel watched the fire, and the flames danced in her eyes. "I wouldn't want to go either." She turned to him. "But you own land. You can do as you wish. It's different for a woman."

A look of utter sadness danced across her face in the shadowy light from the fire.

Christian didn't know what to say. He possessed no comforting words. She was right. Everything was different for him, for he was a man in a cruel world that gave men every advantage.

The soft click of a latch sounded from deeper in the house, and Willem greeted them with a smile. "They're abed. What news of Della?"

Christian shook his head and looked at Mel then back

to Willem. "We have none. Your wife is running to and fro, but no cries came from the room."

Willem nodded then laughed. "I have no idea what that means." He turned to Mel. "Have you ever helped in a birth?"

She winced. "Never."

"Then I suppose we're all best out here caring for the children since we can offer no help inside."

Mel yawned.

Willem cocked his head at her. "Where will you sleep, Ms. Williams? For I doubt there will be any rest in that house."

She tried to wave him away, but another yawn overtook her, bigger this time.

Willem laughed. "I'll go speak with Ivete. They have extra room."

Mel tried to dissuade him, but Willem was intent, and it wasn't until he left that she stopped telling him she would be fine in the main house.

She scoffed at the closed door, her shoulders slumping down. "Do I look so tired? I need not go to bed yet."

Christian smirked. "That nap in the woods really made a difference."

She smiled back. "I guess it did." She returned to her seat and sat down with a huff. "I think I'd rather try my luck in Della's house than cross the prairie at night."

"The prairie at night is fearsome, but a nap in the woods is not? Bears hunt during the day, you know."

She cut him a look. "I did not know, but I told you, that nap was an accident."

He wanted to growl, to tell her he knew precisely why she was falling asleep mid-day... but why would she tell him? He was leaving in a week. There was no reason for her to open herself up to slander, which was surely what she got from her relatives upon telling them her circumstances.

Willem burst through the door, a wide grin on his face. "A boy."

Mel and Christian jumped to their feet and smiled at one another. No matter that this baby wasn't theirs to claim, the joy was infectious.

"Come see." Willem gestured to them and left. They traipsed across the grass to the main house. All was still and quiet in the house now. The buzz of activity had gone. So had Fay and Mrs. Morris.

Ivete held the baby in her arms, a look of utter adoration on her face. "He's perfect," she crooned to no one in particular.

Christian hung back, as did Mel. Willem had told them to come, but he hadn't thought of what an intimate moment it would be for this family to meet their nephew. He didn't belong here. He took a step back and bumped the wall.

Mel gave him a curious look and he tried to smile. He wanted to run away, to hop on his horse and never come back. Mel turned back to watch the sight of Ivete cradling the infant's head, and she squinted at it as though imagining her own babe. Was she glad for it? Did any mother in Mel's circumstances want the baby that grew inside? Had his own mother wanted him? He was most certain that she had not. For without him, her sins would not have been known to the world.

And yet she'd loved him dearly. It wasn't until he was an adult that he realized the start of his life had meant the end to many things in hers. Home. Family. Respect. She'd spent her years with servants as companions, finding joy in her garden and little else. Mel watched Della's babe with such softness, she was naive to what came for her. She had to be. Otherwise she would be sobbing at what the future held—loneliness and shame.

Christian couldn't be there any longer. He stepped quietly away and followed the path to the bunkhouse. He didn't have a light, but that didn't matter. He was used to walking in the dark; he would find his way.

# 15

The Grahams slid into the church pew next to the Morrises. Fay linked her arm with Mel's and whispered, "He doesn't ever stray far from you, does he?" She lifted her eyes to Christian who sat next to Mel.

Mel shushed her friend but kept her face turned toward Fay, so Christian wouldn't see the heat that warmed her cheeks. Christian was handsome. Being hopelessly entangled with another man wasn't enough to blind her to Christian's broad shoulders and striking profile. Or the way his strong hands turned gentle when he dealt with Thomas's livestock. She drew a slow breath, begging her mind to think on a more appropriate subject on this Sabbath morning.

When services were over, Fay pulled Mel away from the group. "He *does* like you. I can see it."

Mel held back a hard laugh. If he did, it was only because he knew nothing of her condition. Fay didn't either, and soon it would be time to reveal all and see if they remained friends.

"Does he have money?"

Mel almost choked. She shouldn't be surprised. Apparently this was the Morris way, to speak freely of finances. "I don't know. He owns something, a house or maybe land too, in North Carolina."

Fay nodded. "He's a gentleman. I can tell. His clothes are fine, and he holds himself in such a way." Fay stretched her neck and looked around the room imitating his serious look.

Mel gave a hushed laugh and glanced at their group to see if anyone saw.

Fay stepped back and looked at Mel's gown. "You dress fine too." She narrowed her eyes. "Are you rich, and you never told me so?"

Mel shook her head. "My aunt and uncle are. They provided all my gowns."

Fay tossed her head. "In a few months' time you'll have plenty of need for all those gowns. Dances will be starting up, and I can't wait to show you off to all the men in the town. You're bound to leave their tongues wagging."

Mel laughed at the image, but she sobered quickly. In a few months' time, she would be visibly pregnant and barn dances would be gone for her forever.

Fay continued. "Though I doubt any of them will hold a candle to Christian. Tell me, why are you not allowing his affections?"

"Fay, you imagine too much. He does not love me. Only we are both outsiders, and I think he feels a kinship there."

Fay lifted a brow. "He's not your kin. What are *you* hoping for? All the Graham men are married, so our only chance for a wealthy one is to marry a guest. I'm hoping for a businessman myself, but if his clothing is any indicator, veterinarians make plenty of money to keep you comfortable."

The Grahams began breaking away from their conversations and moving toward the wagon and horses.

Mel turned to Fay. "I must go."

Fay sighed. "Just as well. I suppose if you rode in our wagon, you'd fall in love with Hugh, and he's much too poor for you."

Mel laughed. Hugh was kind and handsome. He would have no trouble finding a bride, rich or not.

"Don't let him hear you say that." Mel winked and joined the Grahams as they climbed into the wagon and onto their mounts. Though she knew little of horses, she had to suppress a smile as she pictured how they must look riding away. The mounts were large and fine and they made a pretty sight along the road.

Fay was right to hope for a man like the Grahams for a husband. She was pretty, if a bit young to be thinking of marriage. She hoped the men who came were all as respectful as Christian, else Fay would surely be fooled as Mel had been. Only she suspected Della cared more for Fay than Mel's aunt and uncle had cared for her. Fay was at risk of her own heart, but thanks to the affection of the Grahams, her body was safe from the men who might want to use her.

Willem drove the wagon while Mel and Lydia sat in the back with the children. Milo climbed onto the bench seat next to Willem. They'd taken Violet with them to church, hoping to give Della and Bastien a quiet morning with the new babe, Joshua.

Mel remembered the joy on everyone's faces that the new baby was a boy. She'd not been there to know if they had been equally joyed over little Violet. She was certainly beloved, but what was it with men and sons? Were mothers prejudiced to having girls? Or did they too prefer boys? If Mel had been a boy, perhaps her life would have been very different. She might have lived her whole life with Robert's family, gone to university, become self-sufficient. If only she had been a boy.

She touched her hand to her stomach. Did she want a boy? She watched Milo, noticing the way he watched Willem and helped his mother. His helpfulness was more a trait Lydia had taught than something specific to either gender. If she could raise her baby here among these women, she might learn a thing or two on how to raise respectful children, no matter the gender.

Mel glanced up at the riders, Ivete and Thomas as well as Christian, who rode the fine mount he'd brought and would take with him when he left. Heavens, how he looked as though he belonged here. Not like her in her too-fancy frocks and boxes of hats, as though there would be some festivity every other night.

She smoothed her skirt. She supposed if one had to be dressed improperly, it was better to be overdressed than under. And yet, she felt a certain amount of shame, as though she were trying to make everyone feel less than her by dressing above them. And well she might, for the shame would be hers soon enough. As Fay had said, Christian's threads were sleek too, though men's fashion was much less obvious in its finery. One had to look closely to see the wear, or lack thereof, and the smooth weft. From afar, he looked no different than any man in that chapel.

Her cheeks heated again. Christian... in love with her? Silly Fay. What a flattering and amusing comment, but entirely impossible. Yet, she did sense a sort of attention he paid her that he gave no others at Aster Ridge. Perhaps if things were different ... but her earlier thoughts were true. He'd run away if he ever learned the truth about her.

She was glad he was leaving before she could no longer keep her secret. And what of the guests? If she was to abide at this ranch for the remainder of her pregnancy, would they begin to tell the guests that she was merely a widow? A far-off cousin?

She clicked her tongue. More lies.

But what did lies matter next to the sin of infidelity?

Violet climbed onto Mel's lap, and she cradled the little girl, pretty in her ribbons and lace. She was the one person dressed with more detail than Mel, and Mel smiled at the picture she made.

Lydia smiled too. "I think you'll be a good mother."

Emotion overcame Mel, and she pressed her lips together in an attempt to stop the tears threatening to spill.

Lydia sat on the bench next to Mel. "I'm sorry. I didn't mean to upset you."

Mel shook her head. It wasn't a comment that warranted an apology. Mel glanced at Willem and Milo, their backs to the wagon bed. She hoped they couldn't hear. "I've made a mess of everything." Tears fell in earnest at this confession.

Lydia put an arm around Mel and gave her a squeeze. She didn't offer any objections. Not even kind Lydia could deny that Mel's life was now ruined.

"I'll never go to a barn dance." Mel almost laughed at herself, for the words were so immature, wrong even. She'd never cared for a dance, could never get the steps right anyway.

Somehow Fay's encouragement of Christian sliced at

Mel's heart. Men like him, good and kind, could have been her future if she'd denied Luc his desires. If she'd waited for marriage she would have learned the truth and been able to... to... what? Live in a workhouse? Would Robert's parents have taken her back now that Robert was safely married and out of their house? Why had the next place been one of such drudgery and hate. Had they even searched for another option? Or had they merely looked for the easiest place to send her? The path of least resistance. Perhaps she was not so unlike them as she wished. For they'd found the easiest way to rid themselves of her, and she'd done the same for them. Only her way hadn't quite worked out as she'd hoped.

Lydia pulled away and looked at Mel. "You want a barn dance?" Her eyes twinkled. "My husband happens to throw the best dances in the county." She hitched her voice louder. "Willem, darling. Will there be a dance for the guests at the end of the week?"

Mel listened, horrified that Lydia would tell everyone Mel wanted such a thing. It wasn't even appropriate. If there was a dance, she would not in good conscience dance with any of the men. For she was taken, if not by Luc, then by the babe who grew in her belly.

Perhaps in time she could spin the lie of being a widow. A man like Christian might marry a widow with a child. She watched his back as he rode, straight and wide-shouldered. If only she'd met him a year after the baby was born. Or better still, if only *he'd* been the man to come do business with her uncle. If he'd been the one to charm her and put a baby in her belly, he would have had the decency to marry her afterward. She knew it as well as she knew there was a wagon beneath her.

Willem glanced over his shoulder. "I hadn't planned

on it, but if we close all the doors, the barn will be warm. Especially if we've enough bodies to fill it. D'you think the townsfolk will come out on a cold night?"

Lydia smiled. "Folks get restless at the end of winter. They're much more willing to go out in the cold if it means a bit of fun." She winked at Mel. "We will pray for warmth."

FAY DIDN'T WORK on Sundays and Lydia and Mel managed the meal together. Under Lydia's tutelage, Mel was able to be of real use in the kitchen. Lydia did the prep, and Mel stirred or whisked the food as directed. Soon, there was a supper ready for the whole group, the McMullins included.

They were just about done with the meal when a knock sounded on the door. Bastien rose and answered it, appearing again with the midwife close behind.

"And where is mother?" She looked about for Della.

Bastien nodded down the hall. "In bed as you instructed."

Mel smiled at his obedient words. To think such a large man could be commanded by such a short woman with graying hair, though nobody would dare describe her as feeble.

The midwife nodded. "You all eat up now, and bring me a bowl before it's cleared away." Then she disappeared toward Della's room.

Bastien sat again and the meal continued in relative quiet, as though the midwife was imposing and they could not continue their usual conversation. Forks and knives clattered across stoneware, accompanied by a symphony of slurps and sighs, but no one spoke. Mel warmed to think she was no longer the one causing tension in the room. She began to feel very much a part of this little band. Though she supposed she was no more a part of it than Christian, who had been here just as long and was far more welcome when he arrived.

She couldn't help but watch him throughout the meal, and afterwards, as the men sat by the fire. He bounced Violet on his knee. The small girl searched for affection more than ever since her parents had become so distracted with the new babe.

Ivete stood at Mel's elbow. "He's handsome."

Mel jerked and started scrubbing the counter once more. Ivete placed a hand atop Mel's, stilling her from her work. Mel gulped, then raised her gaze to meet Ivete's.

Ivete's eyes were softer than Mel had ever seen them. "You're not dead, you know. Men will look on you with admiration all your life. A baby in the belly won't change that, nor will a child in your arms."

"Perhaps not for you." For Mel, it would most certainly do that. And for a man like Christian, who could have any woman who took his fancy ... she sighed. She would be glad when he'd gone, for part of her knew that no matter how many men traipsed through this ranch, none would make her feel so much regret as Christian did.

The midwife returned and smiled at the bowl on the table. "I thank you." She spoke to the kitchen where Ivete, Lydia, and Mel all stood. "Della tells me there are two more expecting wee little ones. I'd like to look you over. You can sit with me while I eat and tell me all about your condition."

The room was silent. Mel's face burned, but she didn't dare look at Christian. He'd heard. Of course he'd heard.

The midwife's voice was loud enough to wake a babe, loud enough to command a room on how to bring a child into this world.

Ivete came forward with a sad glance at Mel. She sat on one side of the midwife.

"Is it you, dear Lydia? I hoped you'd have another."

Lydia was staring at the woman with wide eyes, her lips moved, but no words came.

"It's me." Mel's voice squeaked. She wanted to say it again, less pitifully, but she couldn't bring herself to speak. Instead, she sat down on the woman's other side.

Willem's voice came from the fireplace. "Let's finish this in our house, give these ladies a bit of privacy."

Mel stared at her hands in her lap. Tears blurred her vision as the dark forms of the men strode past. When they were gone, she closed her eyes and let out a long breath.

It didn't matter. She was shamed, and the sensation was unpleasant, but it wasn't as though she'd just lost Christian. He'd never been hers. He would have always left when the truth was revealed. It was only a matter of time. She knew this, and yet this pain was worse than if she'd said goodbye to him at the week's end knowing she'd never see him again. Now he would remember her with disgust, and it was only this very moment that she realized she'd wanted him to remember her at all.

## 16

The day was warm, and the sun shone bright on Mel's back as she and Lydia worked in the garden. Milo worked alongside them, Willem and Christian having gone to town for last minute supplies.

The guests would arrive tonight. Though she had no idea what to expect, Mel could feel the excited buzz of what was to come. Christian had moved out of the bunkhouse, and when they'd done their work in the garden, she and Mel would tidy it up for their guests' arrival.

"Now that Della's baby is here, are you feeling any more settled about when it's your turn?"

Mel stopped and looked up at Lydia. "It still terrifies me."

Lydia gave her a soft smile. "I don't blame you. Once you get through that first one though, you realize it's not so scary, and it is actually quite exciting."

Mel cocked her head. "You think I'll be having another?" And how did Lydia think she would get another baby in her belly?

"Oh, pish. Of course you will."

Mel turned back to her work. Certainty like Lydia's would be nice. She wasn't sure she would trust a man ever again. The only one she'd be inclined to trust would surely not trust her in return.

She should have looked at Christian after the midwife's fool words. What, exactly, had he felt? Disgust or disappointment? Anger or apathy? She had slept late this morning, partly because she had tossed in her sleep most of the night and partly because she didn't want to face him or any of the men. Though the Graham men already knew she was with child, the shame of it being told so openly still warmed the back of her neck.

Would she lie to him then, her future husband? Would she tell him she was a widow? She knew her letter had been sent, but Luc had still not replied. She needed answers. She was done being moved around. She wanted to live her own life, but she had nothing to her name save a trunk of frocks and hats. She had never apprenticed for a craft. She had nowhere to go.

She kept to her work but spoke loud enough for Lydia to hear. "Where did you go when you were widowed?"

Lydia gave a quiet chuckle. "Here."

"Did you not have family who could care for you and your children?"

"I did, but none so well as Della and Bastien. They had the guest house and Violet had just arrived. They made it sound like they needed me, which of course they didn't. Fay's older sister worked for them at the time. They had all the help they needed."

"And you met Willem?"

She nodded.

Fay's words yesterday were not so far-fetched then.

Meeting a man at this ranch had worked for Lydia, but she was beloved to Della, the matriarch. "Fay thinks she'll find herself a man on this ranch, one of the guests."

Lydia chuckled as she worked. "I wouldn't be surprised. She's a pretty girl, and it's only her family's struggles that prevent her from being the belle of the town."

"I daresay her sights are a bit high. She wants a guest, a businessman to be exact." Mel smiled. Picky Fay. She very much hoped Fay got everything she wanted-- a rich man, fine gowns, and lavish events.

Mel didn't want any of that. She only wanted a quiet house near a good mother like Lydia who could teach her how things were to be done.

---

THE DAY PASSED QUICKLY, for there was much to do. Mel was in the kitchen, helping to prepare enough dinner to feed their usual group as well as six guests. She had just pulled rolls out of the oven when she heard a shout from outside.

Lydia squeezed Mel's arm. "They're here."

Mel's heart beat a little faster. She tried to tell it to be calm, that these guests meant nothing to her. This endeavor wasn't hers. This family wasn't either. But her heart continued its pattering, its foolish delusion. She could argue with it, or go along. Just for a little bit.

The coach was large and could fit more than just the six guests. Hugh and Lachlan drove it, just as they had when she had arrived. The door opened, and rather than a man stepping out, a young woman did. She was dressed plainly, but she had a pretty face. Lydia stepped forward and took both the girl's hands. "Edna, I'm so glad to see you!" The two embraced and Mel looked around for Fay to ask who this was. She'd not expected a woman, only men visitors.

Lydia led her over and smiled warmly at Mel. "This is Edna Archer. She's going to make our lives much easier this week and all the weeks after. Edna, this is Mel, a family friend."

Was she that? A friend to the family? Mel would have thought of herself as foe.

Lydia and Edna talked of Chicago and a bakery where Edna had worked. Mel listened with one ear while she watched men exit the coach. When at last all six guests had disembarked, the coach shifted and one more man stepped out. Mel's stomach turned to ice. Luc Graham.

He looked around as though searching for something. When his gaze landed on her, he cast his eyes down to her stomach. Had he been expecting a rounded belly like Della's had been? His wide smile, the one that had been so charming before, now resembled a sneer, and Mel shrank away from his approach. She turned and fled to the house.

What was he doing here? He hadn't even replied to her letter, but perhaps the letter had brought him here. He intended to deliver his message in person rather than on paper. She gulped and pushed through the front door.

Fay was working in the kitchen. She had not been in the house when the midwife had made her declaration, so she still didn't know about Mel's condition. But now, Mel wished Fay had been there, so she could cling to her and beg her to keep Luc away.

Rather than divulge the news, Mel simply walked through the kitchen and into her bedroom. She shut the door and stared at it a moment before dissolving into tears. The thought of being a mistress had only been words. She could never actually do it. She could never love him again, not now that she knew he was married and a liar. She hated that it was his baby she carried, she'd grown to love the thought of this child who would be hers wherever she went. Now he was here, and she could not forget whose child it was. No matter that she was the one who carried it, was sick with it and tired every day. It was equally his as it was hers.

Had he come here to place some claim on her? To tell her he was going to take the baby after it was born? To raise it as his and Angelica's? Her hands shook, and she clutched them together. She stared at the bed. She couldn't sleep, nor would she go back out and face that group. Lydia and Fay would have to manage dinner alone, although, of course, they had Edna now. Mel had no purpose. She glanced at the window. Could she fit through it? She still wore her jacket; she hadn't stopped to remove it upon her entry. But once through the window, where would she go?

To Ivete's? She must not be expecting Luc. Had she known, she would have been there to greet him.

A soft knock sounded on her door. Her heart galloped in her chest, beating a rhythm she couldn't quiet.

"Mel?" Came a soft voice. Lydia's voice.

Mel opened the door.

Lydia's face looked pained. "Did you know he was coming?"

Mel shook her head. "I sent a letter. I didn't expect him to come."

"None of us knew. He must have figured out the arrangements for the guests and joined them."

Mel nodded.

"Bastien won't let him sleep here, even though they have an extra room. He's going to Ivete's after dinner."

Her stomach flipped, and she thought she might be sick. "He should stay here. I should go."

"Nonsense. There's nowhere for you to go. The bunkhouse is full now, and Christian has moved into the McMullin's empty cabin. If I had a house, I would offer for you to stay." Lydia put a hand on Mel's arm. "You're not going anywhere. You were here first, and you are in a delicate condition. You are our responsibility. Luc will be just fine at Ivete's." Lydia's smile turned wicked. "Although I believe Ivete will give him an earful. If you think you got one when you first arrived, I'd love to hear the tongue-lashing she gives him."

Mel didn't smile. She didn't want to be the cause of discord among this family. They were so close, so loving. Now Luc couldn't even stay with them. "He won't be pleased."

Lydia laughed. "He wasn't. I daresay he feels as the oldest brother he should have deference in all things. But this ranch is Bastien's, and Bastien is as bull-headed as Luc."

A clatter came from farther in the house. Lydia turned toward the noise. "I better help." She faced Mel again. "You don't need to stay in here. He won't do or say anything in front of the guests."

Mel wasn't so sure. She had no idea who that man was. The person he'd shown her had been a lie. If she went out now, it would be the same as greeting a stranger. She sat on the bed with a huff. Her trunks were piled at the foot of the bed, filled with dresses she would soon be unable to wear. Soon she wouldn't be the same woman he'd courted.

So why was he here? There was nothing left between them, except the babe of course. She drew in air through her nose and blew it out through her lips.

Christian hadn't been there to greet the guests. He must be at the cabin by Ivete and Thomas's house. She glanced at the window again. If he didn't know of her pregnancy, might she have gone to him? Begged him to take her with him when he left? Perhaps Fay had been right, and he had felt a shred of affection for her. If only it were more. If only everything were different.

Another knock sounded on the door, soft like Lydia's.

"Come in," Mel called, rejecting her escape plan.

The door opened, but it wasn't Lydia who stood on the threshold. "Good evening." Luc smirked, but his eyes looked hesitant, more so than they had been when he'd stepped off the carriage. "Are you going to join us for supper?"

Mel shook her head, tears burning the back of her eyes as she tried to will them to stay inside.

"I thought you'd be happy to see me. I came to tell you of my plans for you and the baby." He got a goofy smile as he said the last word, as though he got joy at the thought.

"I don't want your plans. I can't trust you." Her words were petty, for she had no other recourse than his plans for her. Her hope was that she could stay here with Lydia and Fay, Della and Ivete. That she could raise her child alongside its cousins with warmth and love.

He stepped into the room and began to close the door.

"Get out." Mel took a step toward him, her finger pointing to the hallway.

Luc's smile faltered, but he continued slowly inching the door closed, watching her as though testing whether or not she was serious.

"I'll scream if you don't get out right now."

Luc froze.

"Now." Mel's voice was low, but it shook. Her hands were shaking too, and she clutched her skirts.

Luc's face turned from confusion to anger. He stepped out and slammed the door behind him. Mel was left to herself again, her chest heaving with the sudden need of air. She went to the window and opened it, leaning on the sill and sucking in the frigid wind. It burned her throat, and as tears fell, the cold collected on her cheeks from the wetness left there.

What had she just done? He was angry. She'd never seen him that way, and it frightened her. Was he going to revoke his family's help? Would he demand she give him what he wanted or be cast out of this house? It wasn't that she wouldn't speak to him at all, it was that she didn't want him in her room. Just because she'd given him allowances before didn't mean she was his forever. She straightened and shut the window. A chill lingered, but she marched out of the bedroom, willing herself to face him, to speak with him where she had the protection of witnesses.

# 17

Christian knocked on the McMullins' door, stamping his feet against the cold. Thomas insisted on feeding Christian so long as he stuck around the ranch to help with Thomas's mare. He also insisted Christian take the mare with him when he left. What would Christian do with a mare that couldn't breed? She was too fine a beast for working in a field or pulling a wagon. Perhaps he could sell her, but he didn't need the money. If he were going to sell the animal, he may as well leave it here.

The door opened and Christian smiled in relief until his gaze landed on the man who opened it. It wasn't Thomas.

"Hello. Are Ivete and Thomas nearby?"

"We're in here." Ivete called, and the stranger opened the door wider still. As soon as Christian stepped through the door and the light hit the man's face, Christian's stomach dropped to the floor. Luc Graham. His face was stern, almost glaring as he shut the door and led the way to the kitchen. He sat at the table as though to finish his half-eaten meal.

Ivete smiled at Christian. "Don't mind him." She glanced at Luc then back to Christian. "He's a bit cross this morning. Christian, meet my eldest brother, Luc. Luc, this is Christian. He will be staying with us for a spell, helping with the horses."

Luc nodded, but didn't look up.

"Grab yourself some breakfast. I'm afraid it's not as good as Della and Fay's cooking, not even as good as Lydia's, but it'll fill your belly just as well." She stuck a plate into his hands and left the house. Her exit was soon followed by the ringing of the bell on the porch. She came back in, blowing into her hands. "It's so cold. This wild country must not know what spring is. I'm sure all of Mel and Lydia's planting has gone to waste, frozen in the ground."

Luc dabbed at the corners of his mouth. "I guess I'm glad you let me sleep in the house instead of the barn."

Ivete cut Luc a look. "I can always change my mind."

Their exchange held more chilliness than the frigid morning air.

Thomas entered, breaking the weighty silence, and greeted Christian with a slap on the back. "Sally's still not ready. I hope we don't need to keep you for longer than a week."

Luc wiped his mouth, the food on his plate devoured. He looked squarely at Christian. Now that Christian could see him clearly, he wondered how he had not recognized the man at first glance. True, he'd only seen him from afar in a dim-lit club, but the man held himself in such a way that made Christian doubt he would ever be able to mistake the man again.

"What brings you to our little valley here?" Luc asked.

"Just a short jaunt before I move east."

"They have you working, I see. They tend to do that." He gave Thomas a sly smile.

Thomas was dishing his own breakfast, and he laughed. "I'm paying him for his work, unlike Willem. The best your brother did was not charge Christian for the use of the bunkhouse."

"I don't mind. It fills the days. If I weren't working, I would have been gone long before now."

"So you came to see Willem's ranch. Was it recommended by someone you are close with?"

Christian shook his head. "Just by a few people around Chicago. I thought I better take a look before I move so far east that it won't be reasonable to visit ever again."

"So you won't be coming back?"

"Likely not."

Luc nodded, as though he accepted this answer as the right one. "Bastien says there's a bear around. All the men are keen on another hunt. Will you two join?"

Thomas shook his head. "I've too much to do, and old Sally could go into labor at any time." He turned to Christian. "But I can help her until you arrive. Would you like to join the hunt?"

"No, thank you. One day in the cold wind was enough for me. Plus, I'd hate to miss her birth. After all, that's why I'm here."

Luc drew his brows closer and considered Christian as though he doubted the words. Christian gulped, shifting under Luc's intense gaze.

Ivete came between them, taking Luc's plate and scraping it clean. "And you, Luc, did you come here to hunt a bear?"

"I came to see how everyone is faring without me."

Ivete's jaw flexed, and Christian watched the two with rapt attention. He knew why Luc was there, and though he now publicly knew Mel was with child, there had been no acknowledgement that he had sorted out who the father was. They would speak in a sort of code so long as Christian was around. He ate faster, trying to look as though he wasn't listening. It wasn't hard. His thoughts were elsewhere, with Mel. What did Luc's arrival mean for her? Would Luc take her away?

Ivete turned and leaned against the counter. "We are doing fine, and you should return to your *wife*."

"I've only just arrived and she is busy enough. I daresay she won't miss me if I'm gone more than a week." His words were a threat, and Christian wasn't sure why. Why would Ivete not want him there? Was it because Mel remained his mistress, and Ivete could not handle infidelity in her sphere? The thought of infidelity, of Mel in Luc's arms, caused his blood to pound in his ears. It shouldn't matter, but he'd have a time trying to convince himself.

Ivete gathered Christian's and Thomas's plates. Thomas reached to take his back, like he wasn't yet finished, but Ivete was already off to the kitchen. The dish out of his reach, Ivete scraped their leftovers into a bowl for the chickens and set the plates in the sink. "I'm going over to Della's this morning, and I don't want to see any of you men there. If you're bored, go entertain the guests. Leave us women alone."

Christian glanced at Thomas, who shrugged. Apparently all men were the enemy this morning.

Christian tucked his lips between his teeth to keep from smiling. "Let's go check the mare." It wasn't necessary; Thomas had just been out there. But Christian wanted to remove himself from Ivete and Luc's line of fire.

As he followed Thomas outside, he asked, "Ivete and Luc have a hard time with each other?"

Thomas slowed to walk next to Christian. "Luc is married to Ivete's oldest friend. He doesn't treat her the way a husband should treat his wife. He and Ivete will forever disagree on that matter. It's just ... bigger than ever these days."

"Because he's the father of Mel's baby?"

Thomas stopped and looked as though he was going to deny it. Then he dropped his gaze and nodded. "She won't like me telling you."

"Ivete or Mel?"

They arrived at Sally's stall and Thomas folded his arms on top of the door. He didn't open it. They weren't truly here to look at the horse, only to get away from Luc and Ivete.

"Neither, I suppose. It's just, this is a family affair, and it's better kept as quiet as possible. If you were going back to Chicago, I might be more discreet, but it's not as though we mean anything more to you than a bit of drama. You're probably glad to be leaving soon, or at least glad this drama isn't what your own family is like."

"My family has plenty of drama." Not even counting his arrival here. He'd say that visit to the law office where he met Francis was enough drama to last him a lifetime. It wasn't bad watching someone else's drama unfold. Only, somehow he was invested. Was it because the people were technically his blood? Or was it that it involved Mel, a bystander who seemed to get bumped by every passerby?

He needed to talk to her, to tell her that what the midwife said hadn't changed anything for him. He hated that her secret had been exposed like that. If he could have foretold the future, he would have told her before, that he knew everything. It still wouldn't have been in her control, but at least it would have been private. That wouldn't have been so bad as her thinking the midwife had spilled her secret.

"I think I'll head over to the main house for a bit."

Thomas gave him an impressed look. "It will be wild. All the children will be inside because of the cold, and the kitchen will be a mess from making food for the guests. The women will be in and out with food and then with dirty dishes."

Christian didn't mind the chaos. It was nothing like he'd ever experienced. It was the bustle of an overfull house, but with it came a love Christian had never known. They might not love him, but he wanted to sit by that fireplace and watch it all unfold. Or help hold a child so a mother could finish a task.

He turned to Thomas. "Your own house will be the same one day."

Thomas grinned. "I hope so."

"How many siblings did you grow up with?"

"Six. And our home was smaller than Bastien's place."

Though the air was cold, Christian felt warm inside. He liked the man Ivete had married, liked everyone on this ranch. They were nothing like he expected, save Luc. Luc was exactly how he expected all Francis's children to be—well-dressed, cocky, glowering. Luc might be part of the family, but he didn't belong at Aster Ridge any more than Christian did. Luc's place was in Chicago just as Christian's place was in North Carolina.

He looked at the mare; there was no way to speed her

along. She would have the foals when she was ready and no sooner. Christian pressed away from the stall.

Thomas smirked. "Good luck."

Christian walked away, unsure what luck Thomas was granting. Was it with the wild house he was headed to, or was Thomas as insightful as Willem and knew Christian had another purpose for going to that house?

———

WHEN CHRISTIAN ARRIVED, he saw the bustle Thomas had been referring to. There was a new girl working alongside Lydia and Fay. Della was in her own kitchen scrubbing dishes alongside Mel.

Della turned at Christian's entrance. "Good morning, Christian. Do you need breakfast?"

He glanced at Mel's back. Her arms still worked on the dishes, but her shoulders lifted nearer her ears. "No, ma'am, Ivete fed us already." He wanted to laugh. No doubt Thomas could use a bit more grub.

"Bastien is out, I know not where, and Willem is in the bunkhouse with the guests. I'm sure you're welcome to join them."

He wanted to talk to Mel, but she kept her back to him and he didn't know how to ask for a private moment with her. Violet came into the kitchen at that moment and tugged on Della's apron strings. Christian scooped the little girl into his arms and walked her into the sitting room. The fire was warm, and Christian sat down with Violet on his knee. She giggled as he bounced her. Then she toddled around, bringing toys over and playing with them on his knee. He watched with a deep sort of content-ment he suspected was a shadow compared to what

Bastien felt daily. Was this how his mother had felt? Or had her feelings been tinged with the stain of his parentage? He sighed, pushing the thoughts away. A weak cry came from the back room and Della dried her hands to tend the newest addition, Joshua. Violet played quietly, and Mel remained alone in the kitchen.

Christian joined her. "I, uh, wanted to talk to you."

Mel still didn't turn. He wanted to go to her, to take her arms and spin her toward him, to meet her eyes and tell her it didn't matter.

The front door latch clicked, and Christian glanced at the entry, waiting for whomever was there to come into view.

Ivete came in followed by Luc, who glanced between Christian and Mel, suspicion clear in his gaze.

Ivete glowered at everyone. "These two need to talk." She pursed her lips and turned to Christian. "Why don't you join Willem in the bunkhouse. I'm sure the gentlemen there will provide plenty of entertainment."

Christian glanced at Mel, hoping she would ask him to stay, but of course she didn't. What had he done to deserve her trust? On the contrary, she likely wanted him there least of all. He nodded to Ivete and left, berating himself the whole time. He'd been so sure about his decision not to tell Mel what he knew, to let her tell him about her condition when she was ready. Now he knew it had been his biggest mistake.

## 18

M el heard the thump of Christian's boots as he exited, leaving her to Luc and Ivete's silence.

Ivete touched Mel's arm. "Why don't you two go sit by the fire. I'll be in the kitchen and do my best to give you privacy."

Mel gave a thankful glance to Ivete. The woman was not perfect. She'd failed to offer proper chaperonage to Mel before, but she'd more than made up for it now with a fierce protectiveness Mel had never known. What would it be like to have Ivete truly on her side? It might be difficult to win over such a woman, but once she'd chosen her fealty, Mel expected it was impossible to turn.

Mel chose a wingback chair by the fire, forcing Luc to give her physical space unless he sat on the floor.

He chose the other chair, and they flanked the fireplace. Mel inched her toes closer, not realizing they were cold until she felt the heat from the flames.

"Will you allow me to speak to you now?" Luc asked.

Mel studied him from under her brows. "It is appropriate now. We are not alone, nor are we in my bedroom."

"You wrote to me, and I came. I would have expected a warmer reception."

"Yes, well, I think we have both been shocked to learn truths about the other." How did this man have so much confidence in his choices that he did not feel a shred of shame now? He'd tricked her, yet he felt no need to apologize.

"I am the same man. I can still beat your uncle at cards and cause color to bloom on your cheeks." He searched her eyes, and it was impossible for Mel to know what he saw there. Did he see forgiveness? She expected he saw exactly what he wanted; for that must be his life, deciding what he wants, then taking it for his own, never experiencing resistance. Heaven knows neither she nor anyone in her family had resisted him.

"You are married," she said.

"I always was."

"If you think it changes nothing, you are mistaken."

"If you think that knowledge changes your condition, you too are mistaken."

Mel clenched her teeth and held his gaze.

Luc tilted his head with a sigh. "I don't want to argue with you. I came to see how you are and plan for the future."

He'd taken her future and held it just out of reach like a horse trainer, waiting for her to perform whatever task he wanted before deeming her worthy of receiving the prize. She wanted to spit at him, like a dusty cowboy leading a wagon. She'd been too long out west.

She turned her gaze to the fire. "I am well. Your family is quite good."

Luc nodded. "I knew they would be. How could they not adore you?"

Mel didn't smile, didn't let the lie tempt her. She'd never been adored in her life. Rather, the Grahams were kind and tolerated her, and for that she was grateful.

"I spoke with Bastien last night. He believes he can acquire us a bit of land. A neighbor down the way is looking to sell."

"The Morrises."

Luc's face relaxed, and a slow smile spread. "You've settled in nicely, and I am glad. Yes, I do believe he said that name."

"Are you looking to buy that piece?"

Luc held her gaze. "Would you like to live there?"

She closed her eyes. She hated every bit of negotiating with such a man. She swallowed the bile that rose in her throat. "What would such a decision cost?"

Luc waved a hand. "Not much, and it would be easily explained to my wife."

"I didn't mean for you. What would it cost me to live there? I'll not be your mistress. You will not be allowed in my home." Mel's throat was dry. The moment had come. Was it now that he would shout? Would he demand she leave his family's home?

But he did neither of those things. He chuckled. "I will not? But it will be *my* home."

"I'll not live there if you feel you can take liberties."

"No?"

She hated his amusement, wanted to scratch it from his face.

"And where will you live?"

She lifted her chin and spoke with all the courage she could muster. "I don't know."

He gave a silent laugh. "You'll live in the house, and I

will grant you an allowance so you might live in comfort along with my son."

Mel felt her resolve crumbling. For she didn't mind suffering for her poor decision, but it pained her to think of her child suffering alongside her. "Will you call him your son? Will he have your name?"

Luc narrowed his eyes, as though considering, but answered too quickly for the pause to have been real. "No. He will have your name and my money."

"And what of your love?" For that was what mattered most. Would her child grow to know a man who neither loved them nor left them alone?

"He will have it, of course. I will visit when I can."

"And you'll stay where?"

Luc laughed, but she heard the note of bitterness it possessed. "With you both, of course. That will be the reason for my visit. I have no interest in becoming a rancher like my brothers. I have no desire to come out to their dust-filled homes and eat with children all around. No, the reason I will come will be to see you and the child."

"You will not stay with us. You may build yourself a home for all I care, but I will sleep alone." For all her days if she must. For as sad as it was to think her days of knowing the love of a man were over, it was sadder still to think of herself waiting for a man to break his vows and come to her. No, she would not let his lie grow. She would not own his lie.

Luc's face darkened. "You seem to believe you have all the choices in the matter."

Mel didn't wait for him to finish speaking. "I realize I have no choices, but I will be on the street before I allow you to mistreat me anymore."

"Mistreat? Darling, I have not treated you ill. I have cared for you better than most men care for their women. I have given you a place to rest, and I intend to give you a better place still, and yet you reject me as though I were some lad vying for your affections with naught but flowers to charm you."

"I am not your darling, nor am I your *woman*." She spat the word.

"You are wrong, for you hold my baby in your belly, and that makes you mine."

"You are married and that makes me no one's." Mel stood, and Luc mirrored the movement, towering over her. The soft noise in the kitchen stopped. One word to Ivete and the woman would come to her aid. Mel wasn't frightened, but she couldn't walk away. Not because of the tall man who stood before her, but because he was right. She had written to him to discover what future lay ahead. She had to work to find the balance. To find how they could both be happy with the reality that was nearer a nightmare than anything else.

"Luc, you will never again enter my bed. I will allow you to see your child, but not for your sake or mine, only so the child may know the love of two parents instead of one. If you do not agree, I will go and find my own way."

"You have no other way." Luc watched her but his expression, finally, held no amusement.

"You are right, and I regret that more than you could ever know. But I am not the first woman to be in this position, and I will not be the last. Those are my terms."

Luc's jaw flexed and his chest heaved with the deep breaths he took while considering. "You'll allow me to have a house built for you?"

"If you vow to me that it is my house and not yours. You must respect my wishes in this matter."

"And how will I see the child?"

"In the yard, in this room ... " She spread her arms out. "At the lake. There is no shortage of space. It should not be difficult to stay outside *my* home." She accentuated the word though it might be pushing her luck. She didn't want him to get any false ideas. He would understand her meaning entirely, or she would leave to face a depressing future, but hopefully a more honest one. She straightened her back and met his gaze.

His face puckered and he glared at Mel. "I agree."

Mel let out a breath as tears sprang to her eyes. She turned to the fireplace so he wouldn't see. She was saved. Her child would have a home where it could live in comfort near cousins and aunts and uncles. It was more than she'd allowed herself to hope for before now.

Luc cleared his throat. "I'll ask Bastien to move forward in acquiring the property for me." He coughed. "Er, you."

Mel pressed her lips together, still barely controlling her emotions. She nodded and heard the shuffle of his boots as he left. It was a different cadence than Christian's steps. Higher, louder. When the door closed she crumpled to the floor, burying her face in her hands. She let the sobs come, though she could not say why she was so overcome.

A hand rubbed at her back, and Ivete shushed her tears.

Finally Mel lifted and looked at Ivete with tight eyes. "Everything is going to be okay."

Ivete nodded, her own eyes so filled with concern, Mel thought she too might cry.

Ivete brushed hair from Mel's face. "It was always going to be okay. Did you think we would cast you onto the road?"

Mel winced, for she had thought that exact thing more than once.

"Mel!" Ivete's voice was hurt. "Don't you know us better than that?" She nodded at Mel's belly, "That's my nephew you carry in there, just as much as if he were in Angelica's belly."

Mel sniffed back her tears. "You all seem so sure it's a boy."

"It doesn't matter, so long as it's strong. The Grahams can't stand the weak." Ivete's eyes held a sort of admiration. "You held yourself wonderfully well."

Mel gave a tear-filled laugh. "I think I need a nap."

Ivete laughed and patted her back. "I'm sure you do." They both rose. "So, did I hear you'll be staying at Aster Ridge?"

Mel thought. "I think I'll be on the Morrises' land, so a bit away."

Ivete scrunched up her nose. "It's no farther than my house. You'll be plenty close, but you can avoid the chaos of Willem's guests. Della is a saint. I know I wouldn't let him overtake my kitchen the way she does." She shook her head and wrapped an arm around Mel. "I'm more sorry than I can say. When you first came, I thought... Well, I was wrong. Can you forgive me?"

Mel nodded. She already had. In fact, Ivete's loyalty to Angelica had only endeared her to Mel instead of the opposite. Ivete stopped at the entrance to the hallway. "Have your rest. I'll stand guard until Della is done nursing the babe."

Mel nodded and continued to her bedroom. Her body

wasn't tired, but her heart and mind were heavy. The thought of Ivete standing guard against Luc, sent her mind spiraling in too many directions at once. Luc had agreed, and yet she could never trust him again. Would he press himself upon her hospitality at every visit? But did it matter? Maybe she would buy a shotgun and ask Ivete to teach her to shoot. She would need such skills if she was going to live alone out west. There weren't as many vagabonds as there would have been a decade ago, but still it wasn't the same as the city where a neighbor would hear her if she called for help.

She tucked herself between the fluffy blankets and closed her eyes. She would have to learn to live alone, for that would be her life. Her purpose was her child, and she would learn to protect her.

## 19

Christian didn't go to the bunkhouse. He couldn't bring himself to converse with strangers just now. Instead, he walked to the barn and stood among the horses. He thought of his first morning here, how he'd found Mel crying. She'd lost that sadness, but Luc's arrival might bring it all back.

He watched the house. When could he go back inside? Was he too late? Had Luc taken his turn to press her for his plan before Christian could offer his own? And what was Christian's plan? To take her to North Carolina and... what? Would he marry her? Could he raise Luc's child as his own? The idea turned his belly. Not because he hated the child, but because he hated Luc. Something about the man rankled Christian, and he couldn't explain it further.

A shuffle of hay made Christian turn to find the very man he'd been thinking of waltzing into the stable, a smile on his face. Christian drew a slow breath. That smile could only mean one thing. He'd gotten what he wanted from Mel.

Christian was too late. Willem had warned him Luc

would charm his way back into Mel's heart. Christian wanted to hate her for it, but he found he could not for he knew how a woman needed the help of the father of her child, no matter their marital status.

Luc leaned against a post and leveled Christian with a look. "How did you find us?"

Christian drew his brows together. "Pardon?"

"Did *you* find my father first? Or did your mother tell you?" Luc's voice twisted on the word "mother," turning it into something filthy.

But that was not the only reason heat flooded Christian, burning his insides to cinders. Luc knew. Perhaps he knew all.

Christian pulled his shoulders back. "I sought nothing. Your father summoned me."

Luc gave a hard laugh. "He did not tell you to come here, so you sought *something*. What do you mean by being here?"

It was a question Christian couldn't answer to himself, and with his blood pounding in his ears, he had even less to offer Luc.

"Are you seeking money?"

"I have plenty of money." He watched Luc, gauging if the man knew of the inheritance that had been granted Christian. "I only came for answers."

"And have you found them?"

He'd seen everyone, met them, and unfortunately, he rather enjoyed all but one of them. "Yes."

"Then be on your way."

Christian shook his head. "I can't. I'm staying for the foals to be born."

Luc scoffed. "I'll pay for the lost foals and their mother. Their lives don't matter so much as keeping my father's privacy." He shook his head slowly from one side to the other. "He would not like you here."

Christian pushed away from the wall. "He has no right to command me."

Luc lifted a single brow. "No? And if he were here right now would you be here too, or would you have scurried off to whatever hovel you crawled out of?"

Christian stepped closer to Luc, his eyes hard. "If I came from a hovel, it was your father's doing and not my own."

"Yes, well, you are an adult now. Go and make your own life, and leave us to ours."

"Yes, yours. I see history is repeating itself in you."

Luc picked at his nails, either unaware or uncaring that Christian's fist twitched at his side, ready to meet Luc's face. Luc crossed his arms. "You mean Mel." He squinted at Christian. "She is no concern of yours."

Luc was right. Mel was nothing to him. She'd not asked for his help, and what could he give her even if she had? A home, perhaps, but would she take it? No doubt Luc had already offered her such, and she had feelings for the man, else her story would be quite different.

Luc uncrossed his ankles and drew a deep breath. "I'm glad we understand one another. There's a town between here and Billings. It's close enough you'll make it before nightfall. Bastien says you have a mount here?"

Christian said nothing, his muscles quivering with the want to tackle Luc.

"Be on your way, sooner is best. You wouldn't want to be happened upon by bandits on your way." Luc turned and breezed from the stable as though he'd just cleaned a whole poker table of their chips.

Christian stood there, his hands balled into fists. Luc's

words didn't matter. His wants didn't matter. Christian followed him outside the stables and was glad to see Luc was headed not for the main house but for the bunkhouse. Christian jogged to the house and burst inside, looking for Mel.

Only Ivete stood in the kitchen.

"Where's Mel?" Christian breathed, no longer caring to pretend he wasn't searching for her.

"Resting." Ivete glanced toward the darkened hallway.

Christian twisted his mouth. Was she always resting? "I'd like to speak with her."

Ivete nodded as she wiped the countertop. "She'll be up soon enough. She had a busy morning."

Christian met Ivete's eyes and held them for a brief moment. The door clicked open, and the sound of several women's voices drifted in.

Lydia gave him a wide smile. "Christian, good morning. I thought we'd see you in the bunkhouse." Lydia turned to the new woman at her side. "This here is Edna Archer, finest baker in Chicago. She's here to see if Willem's endeavor is worth her time."

Edna smiled at Lydia and nodded at Christian. "Pleased to meet you."

Christian gave a quick smile in return. "The pleasure is mine."

Lydia breezed past. "Ivete, you should not have bothered cleaning up. We can do it."

"I know. I had other reasons for lingering in the kitchen." Her eyes flashed to Christian's then away. Was she lingering for him or for Luc?

He turned to go. It didn't much matter anyway. Luc was right. Christian should be on his way as soon as possible. He wanted to stay, to help Ivete with her horses and be with this family for a bit longer, but he was already too attached. He already felt a kinship he shouldn't. It would be better for everyone if he left them to their lives. They'd managed before, and they would do just fine without him.

---

MEL LAY IN BED, unable to sleep. She heard voices from the front of the house, one deep and the other lighter. There was nothing else to discern who was speaking, only that she knew Ivete had promised to stand guard. Or perhaps Della was the one in the kitchen, and Ivete had left her post.

She rose, remembering Christian had wanted to speak with her. Could she go to him now? Was he in the bunkhouse as Ivete had suggested? He knew she was pregnant, and now he knew by whom. Did he know Luc was married? A small sob rose in the back of her throat. What did he think of her? What did it matter?

She rose from bed somehow feeling more tired than when she had laid down. She walked to the mirror and pinned loose curls away from her face. She stared into her own eyes, heaving a sigh for a wasted life. If she'd not been orphaned, she might have used her pretty face to catch much more than an adulterer. She might have found herself an honest farmer. Or a veterinarian.

She cast the thought aside and instead pictured the women on this ranch. She would not have met Lydia or Ivete, Della or even Fay. Christian's face flashed into her mind, but she shook it away. He belonged in the *if* world, not the *because*. He was someone she might have loved if she'd never been orphaned. If she'd been raised in proper society and had a chance to be courted by respectable men. Just because she'd met him didn't mean they were meant for anything more.

She pinched a bit of color into her tired and sallow cheeks and left for the kitchen. From the noise rising from the space, she knew the women who were helping in the bunkhouse had returned.

She smiled at everyone, and when she saw Fay her heart nearly broke. She had to tell her friend. Fay was going to learn the truth soon enough. She'd rather tell Fay herself than let another misspeak do it for her the way it had with Christian.

She touched Fay's elbow. "Can we talk?"

Fay smiled in her young and pretty way, her pink lips full and without pain. "Yes." Her eyes danced as though curious what the fuss was about.

They walked to the entry and both sat on the bench. Mel drew a deep breath and turned to Fay.

Fay stared ahead. "Otto is gone."

The words died on Mel's lips. "Otto. Gone?"

Fay nodded, her eyes sad when they turned to Mel. "Yesterday. Hugh has taken over in the stable." Mel glanced at the door, as though she could see through to the stable where Hugh must be working.

"You must miss him a great deal."

Fay's face twisted. "I should, and I know I will. But besides walking with Hugh this morning, it doesn't feel much different."

Mel nodded and fell silent. How could she burden Fay any more when the girl already bore such a weight? Mel didn't have siblings, and she could only imagine what it felt like to lose one. "Do you miss your sister?"

Fay nodded, "More than I ever thought I would. We fought so much, I didn't appreciate her when I had her."

"I'm sure she misses you too."

Fay scoffed. "Not likely. She's got her man and a babe on the way." She turned to Mel. "They can't ever come back. Della's brother saw to that. I heard he's on a ship down south, joined the navy. I hope he drowns. The turncoat."

Mel reeled at the venom in Fay's voice. At the same time she wanted deeply to hear more about what wrong he had done to Fay's family. Mel shook away the curiosity. "You mentioned your sister is expecting a babe."

Fay nodded and sighed. "Everyone is having them except me." She nudged Mel. "And you."

Mel drew upon her courage for the second time today, feeling the coffer nearly empty. "I'm afraid that is a burden you must carry alone. For I am expecting one as well."

Fay turned to Mel with a look of utter astonishment. Her gaze flicked from Mel's face down to her stomach and back again. "You?"

Mel nodded. "That's why I was sent here. I'll have the baby here in Aster Ridge." Mel thought of the home Luc had promised, of being able to live among these women.

"But ... you've no husband."

Mel shook her head. She wondered what Fay knew about men and women and babies. She was young, and yet she seemed so enamored with men in general. Surely her mother would have taught her a thing or two by now.

Fay studied Mel. "Is it Bastien's?"

Mel's hands flew toward Fay and settled on her shoulders. "Heavens, no. They've only taken me in. It is not his." Mel's voice lost its luster. Fay had not guessed in an entirely wrong direction.

Mel wanted to stop any more questions, so she stood.

"I wanted you to know. Everyone will soon enough, and I wanted you to hear it from me."

Fay stayed in her seat. "I wanted you to go to the dances. You were to be my friend."

"We are still friends." Mel gulped. "I hope."

"Yes, but it will be different now." Fay sighed, as though Mel's condition was a terrible inconvenience. "Can I tell my mother?"

Mel chewed her lip. "I suppose that would be all right. She'll find out eventually."

Fay nodded. She surveyed Mel once more. "A baby." Her voice held a reverence that made Mel laugh.

She wished she could enjoy more of the miracle that was the life inside her. She supposed now that things were settled between her and Luc, she could try a little harder to appreciate what she had rather than seeing it as the end to her life.

The door opened and Christian stopped short inside the frame. "Mel." He looked at her with such an earnest face that she felt herself drawn to him, even taking a step closer. He glanced at Fay and smiled. "Fay. Good morning to you both."

Fay looked between the two, a light dawning on her face. Mel shook her head, but Fay wasn't looking at her. She looked at Christian with such wonder. "You two arrived at the same time."

Mel reached out a hand, "Yes, but—"

Fay smirked at Christian. "I'll leave her to you." Fay bobbed her head and spun on her heel, heading for the kitchen.

Mel turned to follow, but Christian spoke. "Mel, I'd like to speak to you."

## 20

She swallowed, turning slowly. He had that look again, desperation mixed with unease.

"Of course." She made to sit.

He caught her elbow. "Not in here." He tugged her jacket from the wall and held it open. She turned, and he slid it up her arms and set it on her shoulders. She turned and looked at him, waiting for any sort of explanation. He gave a curt nod and opened the door. The air was a wall of cold. She'd not felt it when he'd entered, and her teeth nearly chattered. "We're going out there?"

Christian nodded, with no care for her well-being. She drew a deep breath and stepped into the windy exterior. Christian followed and set the latch, and with long legs he strode to Bastien's stables. Once they were in, the wind stopped, but the air felt just as cold, only now it didn't find its way into every fold of her skirts.

Christian glanced behind him. "I need to get back to Thomas's stable. I don't want them to ride through this just to find me."

Mel nodded. He hadn't seemed to care about *her* walking through the storm to listen to his day's plans.

"I wanted, no, I *need* to tell you. I don't care about the baby." He made a face. "No, that's not it. What I mean to say is what the midwife said"—his throat bobbed—"what your condition is, it doesn't change anything to me. I still admire you."

Mel gave a single, slow nod. What did he mean? Her pregnancy didn't matter? Of course it didn't. She was nothing to him.

"I know it's Luc's child."

She shivered with cold and drew her jacket tighter, relishing the excuse not to meet his eyes. He waited, and finally she looked at him again.

"It doesn't matter. Mel, I care for you, and I don't want you to be in any situation you don't desire."

She surveyed him, not trusting or understanding his words.

He gave an annoyed huff. "What I mean is, I'd like to help. I have a home in North Carolina. I can find a place for you there too if you'd like."

Mel reared her head away from him. Was he propositioning her? Now that he knew she was a fallen woman, he wanted her to live in a house the same way Luc had wanted?

She'd been wrong about him. All men were the same. They only wanted possessions. Carriages, horses, women. Her mouth turned bitter, and she whirled away from him. She wanted to spit words at him, but her throat was too thick with tears. She couldn't summon the same anger she'd given Luc. She'd learned nothing. She'd let another man fool her. She took quick steps away from him, sniffing back her tears.

"Mel," he called. She heard his approach and felt his rough hand take hers. She stopped, wanting something from him, but she dared not acknowledge what it was.

She watched as his hand caressed her own with fingers so gentle, a contradiction to the calluses that he bore. She lifted her gaze to his, but found he too was watching their hands.

He kept his eyes down as he spoke. "I know you care for Luc," he traced the veins on the back of her hand, "but I want you to know you have options. His way is not the only way."

What did he know of Luc's way? Had Christian been listening at the window when they'd spoken? Even Ivete hadn't heard everything.

"I was raised by only a mother." He met her eyes, and his piercing gaze made her feel like he knew her as nobody else ever would. "You are stronger than you think. And I have money." He growled again. "I don't mean." He stopped, drawing a slow breath. "I would never ask anything of you, only I want to make you safe."

He still held her hand, yet he claimed to want nothing from her. She slipped her hand out of his grasp, and that earnestness returned to his eyes.

"You want to care for me, and desire nothing in return?"

He nodded, his exhale a puff of heat between them.

"Why?" If he loved her as Fay claimed, he would offer her something else. But now that he knew of her condition, he must think her tainted. Perhaps he might have proposed something else had he not known. She recalled her face in the looking glass. She didn't doubt his mind might have been moving in that direction. They got along well enough.

"I don't want you to be trapped, to feel you have no choice but to become his."

"You would not have me be his, yet you do not want me?"

The words stung more than they ought. Mel was used to being unwanted. And yet it had always hurt. When would she grow calluses of her own? She ran her thumb along the pads of her fingers. Smooth as ever, though she'd been working this past week. Perhaps it took a lifetime to build up resistance.

"I only want you safe and happy," he urged.

She cocked her head. His words contradicted themselves. No man cared for a woman's happiness. As soon as the thought came, she recalled Willem's attentiveness to Lydia and Bastien's concern for Della as she labored. Perhaps some men cared, but those were their wives. Mel shook her head. She might not have the calluses, but she knew better than to trust a man, a practical stranger, no matter the face he wore or the light in his eyes.

She'd learned how men had wiles stronger than any woman.

She took a step backward. "No." She would not give up the compromise she'd won with Luc. The prospect of living among these women in Aster Ridge, of being happy. She might not have a man's protection, but she also wouldn't have his demands.

She turned and walked toward the entrance again. And if Luc reneged on his promise? Well, perhaps she would have made a plan by then, learned some trade, just as Christian had been encouraging. It was almost as though he'd known she would need some way to live on her own. Like a piece of tinder just lit, the idea flamed up, and she froze.

Had he known? She looked over her shoulder, and he still stood, apparently with no intent to follow her this time. He'd done his fighting, and now he was letting her go.

"Did you know ... about the baby?"

He gave the smallest of nods, as though he was ashamed to admit his awareness.

"Before the midwife?"

"Yes." His words sounded hoarse, like he'd not spoken in a week.

"How?"

"The train. I heard you speaking with your friend."

Mel squeezed her eyes shut. She was a fool. Had she lied to him, spun her own web just as Luc had done? She couldn't stomach deceit anymore. It blackened everything like ink spilled on a page.

"You are right. The baby is Luc's, and I was his mistress. He is married, but I will live on this land under his care and the protection of his family." She spoke the words fast, letting out all the truth before the smallest sliver tried to stay buried. She hadn't been his mistress, not in the way that was expected, but she wasn't about to try to explain and let Christian think better of her. She'd done that too many times in her life, tried her best to be seen the right way by others, to live up to their expectations. It was a relief to know he expected nothing of her, even if it meant she held no respect in his eyes. Perhaps her bad behavior would force him to turn her away now rather than later.

"And that is what you want?" he asked.

"Yes." She raised her chin, but he was too tall, and his height diminished her effort to look down at him.

His stare had gone blank, and he no longer looked at her at all.

She turned and stepped out of the protection of the stable. The wind whipped at her, tearing her hair from its pins.

He jogged after her and came around the front, the wind causing his shirt to billow. "You love him then, even still?" He raised his voice against the wind.

"There is no love in my life." She had never learned love, the giving or the receiving of it. Wind stole the tears from her eyes and ran them along her cheeks into her hairline. "I am a woman and am trapped, as you say, no matter what I choose." She moved to the side, intending to go around him. A gust of wind tore at her hair, tossing it in front of her face and scattering her pins.

He stepped in front of her, blocking her way. "Any woman might be trapped, but I offer you freedom, and yet you choose him. Because you love him."

"I don't." She spat the words, wanting to beat at him with her fists.

He didn't argue, but his silence bespoke his disbelief. Her heart raged, and she stepped around him, putting an arm out to push him away if he dared try to stop her again.

He didn't. It seemed he had said all he meant to say and was through trying to convince her. She entered Della's house, her chest heaving at the cold and the affront of his offer and accusation. His words and intention were as tangled as her hair, and she slumped onto the entry bench where she'd been when he asked to speak to her, the place where her worst problem had been telling Fay the truth.

Her chin wobbled. There was something about Christian that cut at her. She didn't know what it was, but it pained her so much that her throat burned with a trapped sob. She hated being pregnant. Emotions rolled through her like a thunderstorm that had no intention of turning back. She had to wait for it to pass and let it wreak whatever havoc it may.

He'd not offered marriage. Her dreams of finding a step-father for her child were crushed, and not only because Christian hadn't offered, but because she knew by living on Luc's dime, she may not be giving her body to him, but she was giving herself to him in every other way. No man would want a woman kept by another man. That was what Christian offered, to keep her. He also offered the unknown, and she had begun to love it on this ranch. The love that this family shared was unlike anything she'd ever known, and she wasn't going to cast off that chance for her child. Not for anything.

The more she thought, the more decided she became that if he had offered marriage, she still would have said no. She wouldn't risk taking her child from its true family to be set aside when he or she became an inconvenience. She sniffed her tears. No, she would never marry. She would live her life for this child and give it everything that had been denied her, starting with a family who loved and cared for him or her.

Mel drew a shaky breath and stood. She walked to the looking glass and fixed her hair for the third time before supper. She plastered on a smile and joined the women in the kitchen. These were the people she could trust. She would remember that and lean only on them for support.

## 21

Christian watched her go, frustrated beyond his imaginings. He'd often felt frustration with his mother's choice of lifestyle, but never anger. Mel, though ... Mel made him rage. She didn't know what she wanted, only that Christian could not offer it. She must love Luc more than he realized. That thought only angered him more.

He shut his eyes against images of that man's arms holding her, offering her help. Why turn to him when Christian had offered her everything? He'd not made the offer lightly. After all, he had no way of knowing what his aunt would say if he arrived with a woman who was not his wife and who did not intend to become such.

He sniffed. He hadn't presumed enough to think she'd want to marry him, but he hadn't expected such derision, such loathing.

They'd played together, laughed, and when he'd come back for a candle that night, they'd had a moment. What had changed?

Luc.

An easy but unwelcome answer. He exited the stable and rather than follow Mel and hear any more of her rejection, he walked back to Thomas's place, where he was welcome and needed. He'd not set foot in Bastien's house again. He would help with the birth of the foals and be on his way.

———

MEL HAD BEEN MENDING clothes with Lydia when she was sent to the main house for more thread. The latch was already opened, and she only had to push the door to enter. Voices came from around the corner, and she heard Luc's timbre. She stopped. She could leave without being noticed and send Lydia in her stead.

Willem spoke. "She's going to stay here?"

Mel's stomach turned. Willem's voice told her he didn't like the idea of Mel staying. No doubt he thought she would taint his wife and children.

"Just for a time. If I can convince her, I'll move her closer. I don't want to have to come out here every time."

"You'll be visiting?"

Luc laughed. "Don't look at me like that. Would you rather I abandon her?"

"I'd rather you find a way to provide for her and forget about her entirely."

His words hurt. She'd felt a friendship forming between herself and Lydia, but that affection had apparently never crossed to Willem. Did Bastien feel the same way—duty-bound to help his brother but repulsed by the trash Luc left in their care?

She dashed the tear that rolled onto her cheek. With silent hands she opened the door and shut it, not caring if the latch clicked as it closed behind her. Instead of returning to Lydia's home, she ran for Ivete's place, or rather, she ran to Christian.

———

WHEN SHE REACHED THE CABIN, she didn't stop to think, she pounded on the door with her knuckles. They were painfully cold from the run through the cold snap that had yet to lift, and contact with the door made them ache. She shook out her hand and prepared to knock again.

"Mel?" came a voice from behind her.

She turned to find Thomas wearing a look of concern. "Is everything okay?"

She blew into her cold hands. "I'm searching for Christian."

Thomas jerked a thumb over his shoulder. "He's just in the stable. My mare is laboring, but I saw you run past."

Mel worried her lip. Christian was about as busy as he was going to get. Was it truly the time to beg him to consider his offer once more? But he was going to leave when the foals were born. Now might be her last chance. She threw back her shoulders. "I'd like to speak with him."

Thomas shrugged. "I'll take you to him. I hope you're not the fainting type."

Mel entered the stable, and a pungent smell assailed her nose. She covered her mouth and nose and took shallow breaths. "Christian."

He looked up and did a double take. "Mel? What..." He turned to Thomas as though he might explain Mel's presence.

She spoke through her hands. "Can I have a moment?"

The horse lifted its head and stared at Mel with the most unnerving gaze. Mel stepped backward out of Sally's line of sight. The animal lurched and its hooves scuffled on the floor. Christian uttered soothing words and pressed Sally down again.

"Thomas, can you keep her settled?" he asked.

Thomas nodded and traded places with Christian. Christian removed his gloves. Dark stains marked the leather and Mel looked away, pressing a hand to her increasingly unsettled stomach.

Christian's eyes danced with a wary light and he rolled his shoulders, approaching her with hesitating steps. "Nothing has happened at the house, has it? The babe is still well? And all the others?"

She gulped. She should not have acted as though her question was some sort of emergency, but now he'd stopped his work and waited, so she ought to have out with it. "Your offer. Is it too late to accept?"

"My—no." He blinked. "No, it's not too late." His brows knit as though he was trying to puzzle her out.

"I'd like to accept." Mel gave a firm nod, hoping to quell any questions. Perhaps Sally's labor would be just the right distraction to keep him from asking her too many or any at all.

"You want to come with me to North Carolina?"

"Yes, and as I see Sally will be done soon, I can have my things ready to go."

Christian glanced at Sally and back to Mel, his mouth agape. "She's not—you're … sure?"

"Absolutely, so long as you stick to your word that you are not luring me there under false notions." He might give her his word, but she would not believe him. She would keep her guard up at all times, look for a way to live on her own and take it as soon as she found it.

"False notions ... Mel, I never asked anything from you."

"You have acted the gentleman, and so I will agree to your offer."

Sally brayed from her stall, and Mel winced at the sound.

"Christian." Thomas called.

"I have to go. Wait for me with Ivete?"

Mel nodded and turned away from the mare. The two men helping her, was a far cry from Della's labor and delivery. Mel wrung her hands as she put distance between herself and the stable. She would not have those women to help her with her labor. Her heart broke at the thought. They might have wanted to help her, but the men had different ideas. If Mel knew anything, it was that the men had the last say. Their women adored them, and it would only be a matter of time before Willem convinced Lydia that Mel was not the type of friend she needed, that Mel's child was not the type of cousin to be acknowledged.

She climbed the steps to Ivete's home, and instead of knocking she leaned against the wall. She was so tired. Her body, her mind, her heart. Perhaps going with Christian was the obvious answer, and she had merely been too blind before. He proclaimed he wanted nothing from her, and though in the inner most part of her heart she would always wish for him to be hers, she would settle for what he was willing to give. She could be unwanted for just a little longer. Until she found her own way in this hard world.

Rather than knock and stay with Ivete, she turned for Della's house. The sun was setting, and she didn't want anyone to have to walk her home. She was content with having delivered her message. She would pack her things and be ready to leave whenever Christian had the mind to go.

When she entered the house, she saw Luc sitting near the fireplace, his head close to Bastien's in some discussion. She hoped he hadn't already purchased the Morrises' land. Unwelcome as she may be, she didn't want to leave them with any bit of a mess to clean up after her departure. She wanted the women at least to remember her stay with the same fondness she would carry. They were a circle of love, and she was but a pesky fly coming to eat the cream from their labors.

Fay bustled about the kitchen, hard at work.

Mel leaned across the counter. "Did they buy your family's land yet?"

Fay flicked her eyes to Bastien and Luc then back to her dough. "I don't believe so, but Bastien has committed and settled on a price."

Mel screwed up her face. That was before Luc had even spoken with her. So perhaps Bastien was planning to buy the land either way.

Della approached from down the hall, breathing a sigh. "The children are both asleep. I'd love a bit of hot cider before I fall into bed myself."

Fay laughed and opened a drawer, pulling out the rod used to boil water. "The oven is off, but you can hang it by the fire. The men have kept it roaring." Fay wiped sweat from her forehead.

Della returned and reached into the cupboard where they kept the cider. She gave it a sniff and nodded. "It's not hard. Would either of you like some?"

Fay wrapped the dough in a towel and placed her

hands on her hips. "No, ma'am. Hugh is waiting, and he's not as patient a man as Otto."

Della smiled. "Of course. We'll see you tomorrow."

Fay removed her apron and took her leave. When she was out of sight Della turned to Mel. "Would you like some?"

Mel nodded. Perhaps it would soothe her too, and she could fall asleep without her mind thinking too hard about what the morning would bring.

Della poured two cups of cider and leaned her elbows on the counter. "Lydia said the birth gave you quite a fright."

Mel tried to smile. "A bit."

Della nodded. "It's scary, but just remember that women do it all the time. We're made to."

Mel stared into the gold liquid in her cup. "My mother died in childbirth."

Della gave a soft cry. "Oh, Mel. I had no idea. No wonder you're frightened." She set a hand on Mel's forearm.

Mel sucked in a breath, feigning courage. "But you're right. Women do it all the time. She had me without complications. Perhaps it's better that this will be my only babe."

Della quirked her brows. "Your only one? Why?"

Mel shrugged. Did Della want Mel to be Luc's woman? "I'll not marry."

"Ever?"

Mel shook her head. "Who would I marry?"

Della drew her head back. "I'm sure you'll have many vying for your attention. We've a few down the road who need wives. And plenty more in town."

"Not a wife like me."

"You mean a wife with a child?"

"An ill-gotten child."

Della scoffed. "You stop that. You're caught in the dark ages. Men marry widows without much thought, I can't imagine a man would care much about how you got the babe so long as you're faithful to him."

Would that be her way out from under Christian's thumb? She could stay there for however long it took to find a man, kind like Christian, but who also loved her. She could do that here, too—suffer through the men's displeasure at her presence until she found a man willing to marry her. Perhaps she should accept Luc's money and marry one of Fay's brothers. They needed money. Perhaps they could overlook where the baby came from, and the money. If she did that, she could stay near these women. They might be there for the birth of her babe. Her heart warmed, but it was only a dream. She wouldn't overstay her welcome. No, it was best to get going before she was asked to leave.

## 22

Christian smiled wider than the first time he'd birthed a foal. That newness had long worn off, but Mel's acceptance of his offer rang in his ears. Her approach was curious, and he wanted answers, but he wouldn't pry so much that she would deny him again. He didn't think he could take her rejection a second time. He'd tried his best that first time and perhaps she was the type who didn't like a thing unless she thought of it herself.

"I'm going to head in," he said to Thomas. "I need to speak with Mel."

"Will you send Ivete out?"

Christian nodded. He stopped at the pump and scrubbed his hands with the bar of soap, shaking them dry in the frigid air. He breathed a bit of heat into them and marched up to the door. It wasn't until he knocked that dread filled his stomach. What if Luc was inside. He was sleeping there after all, and the sun had long ago set. He tried to gauge how much time had passed since he spoke with Mel, but with the high of birthing those twin foals, he had no way to know.

Ivete opened the door. "Christian, how is Sally doing?"

Christian couldn't hide his grin. "Thomas wants you to go and see for yourself."

Ivete beamed. "She's done it?" She grabbed her coat from the wall and slid into it as she stepped around Christian.

He glanced around the space. It was dark except for one candle that sat next to a chair. A book lay next to it, turned on its pages to hold the spot where Ivete had been reading.

"Mel." He spoke into the darkness, though he was certain she wasn't there. She hadn't waited. He pressed his lips into a line and used Ivete's candle to light a lantern.

Holding it high, he traipsed across the tall grass to the main house. He balked at the prospect of waking whomever was inside, but if Ivete was still up, this household might be too, and Luc must be here for there were no lights on at Willem's place.

He stepped inside and removed his muddied boots. When he came around the corner, Bastien looked up from where he sat by the fireplace and grinned. "How many lived?"

Christian smiled, ignoring Luc's cold stare across the room. As he stepped farther into the space, he saw Della and Mel standing in the kitchen, each with a cup in their hands.

He turned back to Bastien. "All three. Sally did great."

Bastien clapped his hands together and balled them into fists. "That's *fine*. Boys or girls?"

"One of each."

Bastien gave a somber nod. "I suppose we won't breed

the girl, just in case." He cocked his head at Christian. "Not unless we can convince you to stay?"

Christian shook his head, but his stomach dropped to the floor. What would Bastien think when he learned Christian was taking Mel away with him? Bastien was the head of this ranch. If Christian was going to ask anyone for permission to take her away, it would be him. Except Mel wasn't theirs to give or to keep, and giving that sign of respect to Bastien would mean taking something away from Mel.

He turned to her. "Can I speak with you?"

Mel's eyes grew wide in ... what? Fear? She set her cup down and walked to him.

Luc strode forward and glared at Christian. "What do you two have to talk about that you cannot share with your hosts."

Bastien put a hand to Luc's chest. "Brother." His voice growled low, a warning.

Christian looked to Mel, she bit the side of her lip, her face a picture of fear.

Christian faced Bastien. "I'm sure I'll be telling you as soon as I speak to Mel." He put a hand out to usher Mel toward the entry. It was the only spot where they would have a bit of privacy, though he was sure every word would be heard by the people on the other side of the wall.

"You're not taking her anywhere," Luc growled.

Christian sighed. He wasn't about to play cat and mouse with this wolf. Christian raised his brows at Mel. "What do you want me to do?" He wanted to speak with Mel alone, to understand her change of answer, but it seemed like Luc was going to get that answer at the same time.

Christian held Mel's worried gaze. "They're going to know now or in the morning."

The latch clicked and Willem and Lydia came around the corner. They both stopped, possibly sensing the fray they'd just stepped into.

Willem's voice was slow and confused. "What's going on here?"

Luc spoke first. "Christian and Mel have a secret."

Lydia went to Mel's side and glared at all the men, including Christian. He wasn't about to reveal her decision to follow him east. If Mel wanted to join him in North Carolina, she was going to have to find the courage to tell these folks.

Willem turned to Christian, brows raised as though waiting impatiently for the answer.

Christian shook his head. "Mel will say when she's ready. I'll not have Luc force her into anything more than he's already done."

Luc barreled toward Christian, shoving him in the chest. Christian heard a sound like a twig snapping in his brain, and he pushed Luc away. Luc hit the chairs, accompanied by a great screech of wood against wood.

"Stop it!" one of the women cried, but Christian couldn't tell which one.

Blood pounded in his ears, and it was a miracle he'd heard anything at all.

Bastien jumped between them then, one hand against each man's chest. He turned to his brother, his *real* brother. "Luc, go to Ivete's. Mel is not under any threat in my home."

Luc inhaled and exhaled through flared nostrils.

"Go." Bastien's voice rolled low off his lips.

Luc shook his head. "Not until you hear the truth."

Christian didn't take his eyes from his enemy, but he didn't have to look at Mel to know she wasn't going to speak. She'd been trod upon too much to speak for herself now.

Luc nodded a single time in Christian's direction. "He wants Mel. I saw it the first time I saw them together."

Bastien turned his head slowly to Christian. He lifted his brows in the same way Willem had just done, and for a flickering moment Christian wondered if he did the same gesture, if it had been passed down from their father's line.

"I don't *want* her," Christian said, hoping it was right. Mel had likely never had a shortage of men who *wanted* her. "I want to *help* her."

"Help her what?" Bastien spoke more softly now, but his voice still held a note of authority.

Luc stepped back and crossed his arms. "That's not the truth I'm talking about. He doesn't want to help her. He means to make a mockery of our family."

Christian's blood chilled. When he and Luc had spoken, or rather growled at each other about their father, Christian had the impression that Luc wanted to protect his family from the revelation of who his father was. Yet here he was with three of his four half-siblings and all was about to be revealed.

"I never wanted to make a mockery of anyone. I only want to help."

"She doesn't need your help. We are offering her everything here. What would a *bastard* be able to offer anyone?"

The word hit him like a dagger to his chest. He'd heard it often growing up, but it had been so many years, his calluses had been lost and the cut felt new.

Christian felt everyone's eyes on him, but he kept his gaze locked with Luc. He opened his mouth to defend himself, but a voice came from the side.

"Don't you use that word, that hateful word." Mel's voice shook. With anger or sadness, Christian couldn't tell.

Mel's arms hung stiff, her hands balled into fists.

Luc sneered at Christian, an expression of victory. "He doesn't want you. He wants to harm me, to harm our family the way our father harmed him. No doubt he means to take Mel to Chicago and slander my name and that of our entire family. Two Graham by-blows, two generations."

Realization dawned on Bastien's face, and he stepped away from Christian, closer to Luc.

A soft ringing started in Christian's ears, and he took calculated breaths.

"You're our *father's* son?" Willem asked from behind.

Christian turned his head to the side, unwilling to turn his body away from Luc, and nodded at Willem. He raised his eyes and caught Mel's face, no longer afraid, but crumpled in pain. "Mel, I would never do what Luc claims. I have no intention of returning to Chicago for anything."

She dropped her gaze, but not before he caught a lift to her lip. Disgust. She hated him.

The room hummed with unspoken energy, the air around them charged like a bolt of lightning.

The ringing in his ears turned to a buzzing, and Christian wanted to go, but he wouldn't. "I'd like to talk to Mel, alone."

Lydia stepped between him and Mel. "If she wanted to talk, she would have."

Christian wished it had been any of the men in the room to speak those words. He couldn't rage at Lydia the way he wanted. "She did want to before Luc spewed lies."

"The lies are yours alone." Luc spoke with the drawl of a winner wishing the loser better luck in the next round. Christian looked at every face in the room, each of them against him. He turned and brushed past Willem as he went outside.

He stalked to the stable and pulled Blue out of his stall. He readied the horse with quick fingers, the way he used to when he was a child and had been waiting all day to ride. Just as he set the saddle on Blue's back, he heard someone approach. He didn't turn as he spoke. "I'll be out of here as soon as I can get my things. I'll find a place in Dragonfly Creek."

"Does Ivete know who you are?"

*Willem.* Christian froze. "No."

"Why didn't you say anything?" Willem huffed a laugh. "I can see it now. I'm surprised none of us saw it before."

"I never planned to stay this long. I only wanted to see you, to meet you."

"But you stayed."

Christian swallowed and started in on the saddle, tightening the girth and tucking it into place. "I only wanted to help where I was needed. I didn't plan—" His words sounded weak. If he'd truly wanted to go, he would have gone.

"Did you stay for Thomas and Ivete or for Mel?"

Christian slapped his thighs. "I don't know. Both. Neither." He lifted his face and stared at the rafters.

"She was going to go with you."

Christian barked a laugh. "She won't ever trust me now."

"I suppose a girl who's been fooled once doesn't trust easily. You broke that trust."

Christian leveled Willem with a stare. "You can't break what isn't there."

"Her face said differently."

Who was this man? Why did he want Christian to hear these things? "It's done. I'm leaving." He stopped and stared at Willem, so like himself in many ways. "I'm glad to have met you."

Willem nodded. "Same."

The two clasped hands in a firm shake. Willem said, "I don't know that you should go by Ivete's tonight. I can bring your things to town in the morning."

Christian nodded and climbed atop Blue. He clicked his cheek and the horse stepped around Willem and into the chilly night air.

## 23

Mel watched as every head turned from the door where Christian had disappeared and, one by one, rested on her.

She swallowed. "I—" She tucked her lips between her teeth. She had nothing to say. She'd betrayed their trust, rejected their hospitality—forced as it was. She'd thrown everything in their faces as though it was feed for the chickens. "I'm sorry."

Lydia stood at Willem's side now, no longer a protective force in Mel's favor. Mel was a fool, and she knew it. Now everyone else did too. Once again, she'd trusted a man, only to be torn in two at the hidden truth. As though her humiliation wasn't great enough already.

Bastien spoke, his words breaking the thick silence and causing Mel to flinch.

"Luc, it's time you went back to Ivete's."

Luc hesitated only a moment before conceding. Mel glanced at Bastien. Why had he sent Luc out right after Christian? Heaven knew those two weren't done with each other yet. Willem must have had the same thought because he turned and followed Luc out of the house. The door clicked closed.

How long until everyone left her alone with her shame? Or would they ask her to go? Would she be forced to leave with Christian now that she'd been shown to favor him over Luc? Had he really planned to flaunt her in Chicago?

"Do you want me to go?" She spoke quietly. Their answer could mean death. It was too cold to be turned out without a plan.

Della huffed. "Of course not, darling." She came to Mel's side and squinted at her. "Do you really think so little of us? It's no wonder you wanted to leave."

"I didn't—I don't think *little* of you. You are all the most wonderful people. I only meant to remove my stain from your beautiful place." She glanced around the space from the beams in the ceiling to the wood on the floor. "I don't belong here."

Lydia leveled Mel with a look. "You belong here more than you belong anywhere. Who said you were a stain?"

Mel didn't want to cause trouble for Willem. "I'm not the sort that you folks should concern yourselves with."

Bastien crossed his arms. He frightened her on the best of days, and today was not one of those. "Luc's made sure we are concerned. Now there's no forgetting you. No more talk of leaving. It's late. We can talk in the morning."

The three women all exchanged glances. Mel obeyed Bastien's order first. After all, if she was allowed to stay, the last thing she wanted was to go against her host's wishes.

She shut the bedroom door behind her and pressed her fists to her eyes. In trying to fix things, she'd made them worse than before. The same as she'd done when she'd been living with her aunt and uncle and she'd given

Luc hope. She'd thought to fix her situation. To marry a man of wealth and charm.

Christian was wrong, she wasn't good at a single thing. She bungled everything. The babe in her belly would one day realize what a curse it was to be born to Mel. She crawled into bed without removing her dress. She tucked herself under the covers without a care for wrinkles or comfort. She only wanted to close her eyes and forget everything.

---

CHRISTIAN RODE for Dragonfly Creek at a trot. He had no care for holes and almost wished for his horse to catch one so he might be thrown. At least then his body could experience a pain equal to what gripped his heart. When he arrived in Dragonfly Creek, he found the only inn and paid for a room with coin from his saddlebag. He fell into the smelly sheets and closed his eyes, but sleep did not come. What was Mel facing at the ranch? Had she told them everything or let them believe Luc's fool words?

It didn't matter. The more important truth was out, and they would think what they wished.

Only it did matter what *she* thought.

Only an hour ago, elation had coursed through him. He shook his head. The live foals had been exhilarating, but they were nothing compared to the prospect of taking Mel to North Carolina. His mind had spun, considering the future. He thought he might have won her heart. It wasn't until she opened up that tiniest of spots that he'd allowed himself to hope. He had imagined they would continue to find her hobbies, to try out everything, be it interesting or not, until they discovered what she loved.

He wanted her to have something for herself, so that even if she never had to work a day in her life, she had options and never felt trapped again. It was more than an attempt to correct his mother's prison. He didn't just want Mel free, he wanted her happy.

He scrubbed a hand over his face, his whiskers whispering against his palm. She would be happy enough. Perhaps not as happy as he might have made her, but that was lost now. Luc had ruined their chance, or perhaps he'd only rushed them forward to a future when Christian would have felt the need to tell her his parentage. His relation to the Grahams, and even to the babe she was carrying. She was right to not trust him. He wasn't honest. Not since he'd come to this ranch. Why had he felt the need to keep his father's secret? Had he been protecting his father or himself?

---

MORNING DAWNED and though Christian hadn't been able to sleep, he also couldn't rise. His heart felt as heavy as his legs, and he lay in the bed, staring at the window as it brightened with the rising sun.

He wasted the morning away eating breakfast from the inn's kitchen, which tasted like ash— whether from his state of mind or from the chef, he didn't know. Finally, Willem arrived with Christian's things from the McMullins' home. Christian met Willem on the road. Willem had brought only a horse with a bundle of Christian's belongings.

"Who is tending your guests?" Christian asked.

Willem waved away Christian's concern. "Hugh is with them in the woods, teaching them to set traps. I doubt we'll catch any martin this late in the season, but they can buy a fur off Hugh if they're so inclined." He climbed down from his horse and passed the sack to Christian.

"Thank you." Christian met his half-brother's eyes and tried to say everything with a look.

"Ivete is none too pleased that you're gone."

Christian knit his brows. "Does she know?" Of course she knew he was in town. That wasn't the question Christian was asking.

Willem chuckled. "Not because Luc said anything. I think he would have kept you a secret his whole life through. No, she wanted to know why I was gathering your things, why you were leaving so abruptly." He smiled at some far off memory. "You should have heard the licking she gave Luc. I thought her voice might break. I haven't heard her rage like that since we were kids and I cut her hair."

Christian wished he had been there, not to witness Luc's disgrace, but to take his own punishment. For he had also witheld truth from Ivete. He ran a hand through his hair. "Is she okay?"

"Ivete? She's fine. Or do you mean Mel?"

"Both."

"I can't say how Mel is, haven't seen her today."

Christian wanted to return, to plead with Mel, to tell her all the truth and let her decide which future she wanted.

"I would have taken care of her."

Willem shrugged. "She'll be cared for."

He was right. Mel would have food, clothing, and shelter. "But what about freedom and love?"

"Love goes two ways. I think she'll find we care for her more than she realizes."

"But she'll never be there on her own account. I wanted *her*. The baby ... it would have been welcome too."

"You would have raised a Graham child?" Willem cocked his head slightly and gave Christian a curious look.

"In time I think she might have let me. Might have been able to trust me enough to love me."

Willem rolled a rock with the bottom of his boot. "Could you still convince her?"

Christian quirked a brow. "Not from here." He thought of how he seemed to always bungle his words with her. "I'm no good at writing letters." He met Willem's eyes, and the man's silence felt weighted with something. "Will you take me to her? Help me see her alone, so I might speak to her?"

Willem laughed. "For knowing us less than two weeks, you sure have the right of it. Would you have asked Bastien if he'd been the one to deliver your things?"

Christian wouldn't have asked Bastien. There was something too serious about him. He didn't seem the type to take a risk like this.

Willem smirked. "What about Ivete?" He narrowed his eyes at Christian. "I think you might have been able to pull her into your plan."

"We still might need her. Mel won't go anywhere alone with you."

Willem gave a thoughtful nod. "What's your plan?"

## 24

Mel worked at Fay's side all morning. She kept her eyes down and hated herself for the way she'd treated the Grahams. If she'd actually left with Christian, she would have treated them equally ill, but she wouldn't be here to feel the effects of that treatment.

Fay had been watching her all morning, and finally the girl took Mel's arm and spun her so they were face to face. "What is going on? This whole household is walking around like they're crossing a creek on a fallen tree."

Should she reveal Christian's relation to the Grahams? That might be something they'd rather keep to themselves. "I had thought to leave with Christian today."

Fay's jaw dropped, then the corners of her mouth lifted in a smile. "You sly thing. I knew his heart was yours, even before" —she flicked her gaze to Mel's stomach—"I knew."

Mel shook her head. "He wasn't mine. Not like that. The baby is Luc's. Christian only wanted to help me. He knows about the babe, about Luc."

Fay shook her head, apparently taking the news about

the baby's parentage without second thought. "I have brothers. Men don't help women without love in their hearts." She laughed. "It has to be the right type of love, for my brothers don't seem to mind letting me haul wet laundry to the line, no matter how much it weighs."

Mel tried to recall Christian's invitation. "No. He made it clear it would be nothing like love."

"Perhaps he was afraid you'd reject that. Was he playing to your logic?"

She truly couldn't remember. Everything was muddled. When he'd first asked her to go east with him, he'd spoken of want. She'd thought he'd meant in a lustful sense, the same way Luc had wanted her, but what if he'd meant something else, something closer to the heart?

An image of how she'd last seen him —with a stricken face as he rushed from the house, his parentage and lies revealed to all— tumbled into her mind. He'd seemed so sad. But why? Because he'd been found out? Or because ... because he'd lost her?

"It doesn't matter now. He's gone and his offer left with him."

Lydia entered the kitchen with little Bridget on her heels. Fay gave Mel a sad look and a silent nod, then turned back to her work.

Lydia leaned over the counter and asked, "Fay, would you watch Bridget for a bit? I need to speak to Mel."

Mel straightened and met Lydia's smiling gaze.

"Of course." Fay walked over and tousled Bridget's hair. "Shall we bake some cookies?"

Bridget's face lifted in a huge smile, and Lydia nodded at Mel. She walked back to the front and took a wrapper from a hook and passed it to Mel. "You'll want this. It's chilly out."

Mel accepted the scarf and wrapped it around her neck then put her coat over top. Lydia took another wrap and did the same. As Mel followed her out of the house she became certain they weren't stopping at Lydia's home. They were too bundled for that.

Lydia linked her arm with Mel's, and they walked side by side through the grass, passing the garden.

Mel said, "Will the seed we planted make it through the cold?"

Lydia pursed her lips. "I hope so. They should be fine, but this is a mighty cold snap. Let's just hope it's the last one before the cold leaves for good."

Mel looked at the valley and tried to picture it dotted with wildflowers. "How did Aster Ridge get its name?"

"If you stick around, you'll see."

Mel nodded. She would see. But why did it feel like a snare gripped her ankle? Bad as she would feel for rejecting the Grahams' offer of shelter, part of her wished she could go with Christian, to live the life he had painted in her mind. If Christian had not planted that seed in her imagination of a now-dead future, would she have begun to feel trapped as she did now?

It was foolish to miss the opportunity. She could do everything he suggested here in Aster Ridge. She could discover her talents, learn some trade so she could support herself. Or, like Lydia said, marry someone from here. Just because she stayed, didn't mean Luc owned her. She tried to picture the man who would be bold enough to marry her knowing she lived on Luc's dime. The only man she could picture was Christian, and he wasn't bold. He was only cunning.

Lydia squeezed her arm. "Are you thinking of Christian or Luc?"

Mel laughed. Was she so easy to read? "Both."

"Do you love him?"

She might have loved Christian if they'd met under different circumstances, if she hadn't already learned that to love was to welcome melancholy into one's life. "When Christian made me the offer, he didn't speak of love. I don't think he meant to do what Luc claimed either. He wasn't going to traipse me through Chicago and ruin your family's reputation."

"I don't think so either. Though last night when Luc said as much, he somehow knew how to hit on everyone's fears."

"Why did Luc not say anything earlier? Would he have kept Christian's secret if I had never threatened to leave?" A gust of wind swept across the prairie whipping their hair against their faces. They'd passed the buildings now and must be headed for the lake.

"Probably. Willem thinks he had been keeping the secret long before he arrived in Aster Ridge."

Mel shook her head. Luc's possessiveness had caused him to reveal a secret he'd kept for who knew how long. Would she truly be free to live her own life, to marry, if a brave man came along? Or would Luc ruin everything every time?

"So, Christian's getting too close to me was what got him in trouble."

"I suppose so, but he was the one to tell the lies. I'd say he's not totally innocent in this."

Mel imagined her own child, living in a world with no siblings, only to learn he had some. "I cannot blame him for wanting to meet everyone."

They crested the ridge, and two figures mounted on horses stood at the shoreline.

"I'm glad you don't feel anger toward him, for he's come to speak to you, and I hoped you'd not be cross with me for bringing you here."

Mel stopped walking, and because their arms were linked, she forced Lydia to a stop as well. "That's Christian?"

Lydia nodded.

Mel glanced over her shoulder, as though Luc would come up behind them and boot Christian from the property.

"Willem brought him here?"

Lydia nodded again.

Mel remembered Willem's words to Luc when they were alone in the kitchen. "He wants me to go with Christian, to leave here." That thought, though it had once made her believe she didn't belong, rooted her to the ground.

She wanted to stay. To see the asters bloom. She wanted to give birth to her baby here, with these warrior women around her, to raise that child in this valley with its cousins. But they wanted her to go. Willem surely did and now Lydia. "You want me to go?"

Lydia grabbed both Mel's arms. "I want you to be happy. I don't want you under Luc's thumb. He's too... convincing."

"You think I'll become his mistress."

Lydia winced. "I don't know that, but I think you won't have the luxury to do what *you* want."

"And going with Christian will give me ultimate freedom?" Mel shook her head and backed away. She glanced at Willem and Christian. They both faced her now, probably wondering why she and Lydia stalled on this hillside.

"He will love you as Luc never can."

Mel took another step backward. "He doesn't love me. He only wants me to choose him over Luc." As she spoke the words the idea blossomed in her mind. This was some sick wish fulfillment from Christian being rejected by his father. Or perhaps it had to do with the babe in Mel's belly. Christian wanted to control Luc's child.

Convinced, Mel turned around and hiked back up the hill. The sound of hooves thundered behind her, and she broke into a run. She didn't want to face him, to hear any more convincing words. She wasn't wanted here, but she'd been prepared for that outcome her whole life. She'd been taught to stay for the benefits and endure being a nuisance. The benefit would be to her child, and she would stay. Nothing Christian could offer her would make her leave this place. This was where her baby belonged, and if it meant she lost a few freedoms, so be it.

"Mel." Christian called as his horse came along her side.

She barely looked at him and kept running.

The horse passed her, and Christian reined it to a stop. He slid down in one motion and stood with the reins in his hand, waiting for Mel to run to him. She veered, intending to go around, but Christian dropped the reins and ran after her.

She was no match for his long Graham legs, and he caught her in his arms.

She beat against his hold and shrieked at him. "Let me go!"

She writhed in his grip and felt herself being lowered to the ground.

He loosened his hold and took her by the arms. He put his face close to hers. "Are you afraid of me?"

She jerked and turned away. Tears poured down her cheeks, and she couldn't say exactly when they had started. "What do you want?"

"A word with you. I cannot leave until I've spoken with you."

Her legs pulsed from the effort of climbing the hill to the lake then running back up that hill. Her body weakened in his grip. If he hadn't been holding her up, she might have collapsed to the ground.

"Why did you accept my offer?"

Mel watched his lips move. She didn't dare meet his eyes. "I don't accept it."

"But you did, and I can't leave until I know why."

"Because I'm not wanted here, and I thought maybe you did want me there."

"I did. I *do*. Come with me."

Mel shook her head.

"Why not?" He squeezed her arms as he asked, his voice pleading.

"I want to stay."

"Because of who I am? Could you not love someone like me?"

Mel's intent to not meet his eyes crumbled. Her gaze flew to him. "Love you?" Her mouth opened and closed wordlessly.

"Is it that you can do better? You wish for someone who wears his father's name."

Rage boiled in Mel's gut. She pushed at his chest, but his hold stayed firm. "You think you are less because you have no father?" She pushed him again, but he pulled her back, closer this time. "Will you think the same of the baby in my belly? Will you think she is less because she has no father?"

"I'll be her father. I'll care for you in a way Luc never could."

Mel surveyed him. "I cannot tell who you hate more. Luc or yourself."

His face crumpled.

Mel watched with a disconnected interest. "Is your intent to take me from Luc?"

His eyes held fire as he said, "No."

"And you want me to love you?"

His face contorted with pain. "I had hoped love might come."

"But you could love *me*." Mel wanted to shake her head, to stop this foolish dream from playing out in a way that she would never be able to forget it when she woke.

He nodded, but his eyes held more than promise, they held truth.

"Do you love me already?"

He held her gaze for just a moment before he gave the tiniest of nods.

"How?"

One hand left her upper arm and brushed a lock of windswept hair. "Are you not aware of the effect you have?"

Mel thought of Luc. She'd thought for a moment she was capable of catching the best of men. "Any effects I might have do not serve me well." Then she thought of this place, of the people she'd met, the love she'd felt from some and how it countered the words she'd heard from Willem.

"You have captured my heart."

Mel shook her head. "I have ignited a lust, a desire to take away from this family who has everything."

"I don't mean to take you away from them, only to provide a life worthy of you."

Could that be true? She studied his eyes. His brows angled with an earnestness that warmed her heart. She'd never been wanted. Not like this.

"I could love you." A wave of relief crossed Christian's face. Mel yearned to touch it, to run her finger along the dark stubble of his beard. But she couldn't, not until she knew. "Could you stay here?"

He blinked. "Here?"

"Here." She watched him closely, waiting for his rejection, for him to tell her she wasn't worth the contention that would exist if he stayed here with her.

He shook his head, blinking. "You could love me?"

"I could."

"You won't leave?"

Mel shook her head.

"What is here if it is not Luc?"

"I love it here *despite* Luc. I love everything. The lake, the hills, the homes, the hearts. I've never felt part of a family the way I do here."

"If I were a Graham, I would give you a life here."

"You are a Graham."

"I am a Milnes. I don't own anything here."

"I heard there's a bit of land for sale."

He searched her face. "If I stayed, would you stay with me? Marry me. Let me love you with only the hope you might love me in return."

The breath was stolen from Mel's chest. "Marry you?"

"Please, Mel. I love you. I have since you spoke nonsense to the horses while I cleaned their hooves."

"And what about the day I make you angry?"

"You *have* made me angry."

"When?"

Christian shook his head. "Don't push me, woman. You're making me angry now. Will you give me an answer?"

"You propose marriage?" Mel wasn't sure why she felt so disconnected from his offer. In many other scenarios she would have been thrilled to have such a proposal. And yet, she felt as though she were watching another woman being held by this perfect man. This man who was both strong and kind, truth and lies.

Christian let go of her arms and raked his hands through his hair. A few strands fell onto his forehead, and she reached up to brush it back. After she'd done so, he caught her hand and pressed it between both of his.

He looked at her with earnest eyes. "If you'll but give me hope, I'll wait for your answer. I'll stay in town, find us a house there and you can send for me whenever you've decided."

"I don't want to live in town. I want to live here."

"In Dragonfly Creek."

"In Aster Ridge."

His eyes flew wide and he coughed. "I don't—Aster Ridge is Bastien's."

"You could buy the Morris land."

Christian looked out over the land as though the dips and valleys held his reply. "If I did, would you say yes?"

Mel nodded. She watched him, waiting for doubt. Waiting for him to tell her she asked too much and he didn't love her without restraint.

He spoke slowly as though whatever he was trying to work out wasn't yet complete. "I want to speak to Bastien first. And Willem and Ivete."

It was Mel's turn to reel at the request. "Why?"

"I'll not live in their valley without their permission."

"But you would live here?" She couldn't keep the incredulity from her voice. Did he not care that Luc was bound to visit? What of the claim Luc might make on her child. Had Christian thought through all of this already? Or none of it?

"Tell me why you want to stay. Convince me." His lips held the faintest smile, and his eyes never left her. The way he watched her, she felt as though she were sitting for a quiz back in Hannah's schoolroom.

There was a beat of silence, broken only by the whistling wind. Mel sniffed, the cold making her nose run. "I've never been to a place like this. So full of family ties. I always thought the closeness of siblings died with adulthood. But they prove otherwise. I think my relatives were just a certain sort."

Christian harrumphed like a grouchy man. "They must have been something." His face softened and he took her hand. "If we marry, I will be your family. Do you want that?"

She nodded and by the chuckle he let out she had done so quite vigorously.

A look of amusement crossed his features. "Your relatives ... would you like me to ask someone for your hand?"

Mel blinked at him. What man was there to give her away when no one claimed her to begin with? "No. But what will you do if Bastien doesn't want you to live here?"

Christian worked his mouth. "I suppose that's up to you. If they will let you stay and not me, then the choice becomes yours once more."

Mel liked that idea, having a choice. She felt a power rise up that she'd never before known. She might still be a nuisance to the Graham family, a black mark against their brother, and yet with Christian she was something else. It wasn't that he would cow to her, but rather that he wanted her as nobody had ever wanted her before. He didn't want her body like Luc, or accept her due to familial responsibility. He wanted her to have what she wanted, and the sensation was unfamiliar.

She cocked her head at him. "You don't mind not having a choice?"

"I've made my choice." His eyes were bright and a small smile played on his lips.

Her throat burned. Why had he never looked at her that way before? If he had, she might have begged him to take her to North Carolina. They would have told the Grahams together and Christian would stand with broad shoulders and take whatever they wanted to pile onto him. Be it words or blows. He was willing to do so now.

"You are not afraid to talk with Bastien?" She glanced down the hill to where Willem and Lydia stood near the horse, their heads bent together.

"I'm not afraid."

"Why didn't you tell them who you were?"

Christian drew in a deep breath and let it out slowly. "I didn't plan to say anything, not for my own sake, but because it would do only harm." He drew a breath. "To everyone." He shrugged. "Now the harm is done. A bit more shouldn't break the horse's stride."

She leaned closer, letting his back block most of the wind. They were curled closer to each other now, as though through their words, their bodies, and their hearts had drawn together.

He'd hidden the truth to protect his half-siblings. Mel glanced up at him. "Do you think it will cause them more grief?"

"We're certainly not making their lives easy, but if you want it so badly, I think it will work for the good in the long term."

Her brows twitched. "You trust me so much?"

He smirked. "I can see what you mean, about family. They don't think of me as such, but you" —he gestured to all of her— "you fit right in with those women."

His exaggerated words warmed her. "Not more than you do with the men. You resemble them, though I cannot say exactly how. Perhaps it is only your height, but it's also in the set of your shoulders." She shivered.

"Can I take you to the house, warm your hands by the fire?"

Mel nodded. They stood, and Mel shook out her skirts just in time for Christian to lift her onto the saddle. He climbed up behind her and settled her against his chest. His warmth seeped through her jacket, and her eyes grew heavy with fatigue or contentment, it was hard to decipher.

"I do not remind you *too much* of them ... of Luc?"

Mel turned her head, but she could only see his shoulder out of the corner of her eye. In all her imaginings she had never thought to marry a man who truly knew her circumstances. She'd thought of claiming herself a widow, but didn't expect a man could love her despite knowing her history. She tucked her head tighter against him. "No. You are nothing like him."

He slid a hand from where it held the reins and settled it across her stomach. "Will you let the babe take my name?"

Twice over it should have been named Graham, and yet, she loved the idea of her baby being a Milnes. "I'd love that more than anything."

He must have been as content as she because they rode the rest of the way in shared silence. She leaned against him, riding the high and low of his breathing and syncing her own to match.

By the time they arrived at Bastien and Della's house, she wasn't cold any longer. Christian climbed down and reached up to help her. He'd only just set her feet on the hard ground when Luc's voice greeted them.

"I thought I saw a snake slithering through the grass."

Christian put a hand on Mel's hip and guided her behind him. "I'm here to speak with Bastien."

Mel stared at Christian's back, afraid for him. Why had she made her answer dependent on whether or not he would stay here? It had been an unfair demand. Now he faced Luc without the confidence to know she was his no matter the outcome. Could it be that their conversation, that contented ride, had changed so much for her? She wanted to live here, yes, but not if it meant losing Christian. She wanted those arms around her, his wide shoulders standing between her and the cruel world. She wanted her baby to have his name. She wanted to carry his children in her belly.

Willem and Lydia arrived and dismounted from Willem's horse. Lydia took the reins from Christian's hand and gestured for Mel to follow. She stood for a moment, unsure whether she should stand by her man or whether he would be better off without her near.

Christian turned his head. "Please go with Lydia and Willem."

Willem didn't look as though he was going anywhere, but Mel didn't argue. She caught up with Lydia as she walked the two horses into Bastien's stable. Lydia threw

Blue's reins over a post and walked Willem's horse a bit deeper into the stable before doing the same.

"Shouldn't we be out there?" Mel watched the entrance, miffed that she wasn't able to see them from where she stood.

"In my experience the men are best left to their own devices."

"Even if it means they will beat each other to a pulp?"

"Especially so."

Mel spun and looked at Lydia with confused regard.

"You'll understand more when you have a few little ones." She didn't bother unsaddling the horses. Perhaps she wasn't sure whether Christian would be staying or going. She waved Mel along and turned toward the back of the stables. "C'mon. We'll go around the back of the house."

They walked past the very spot Mel had taken refuge that first day, where Christian had found her and made light of the mouse in his cabin. He couldn't have loved her yet, but he'd treated her well even then. She recalled his revelation. He *had* known then what her condition was. She wanted to relive everything with this new lens, to hear every conversation in a different light. A light that wasn't marred by her deceit.

"He's going to ask Bastien about buying the Morrises' land."

Lydia turned, shock plain in her wide eyes. "To live?"

Mel cringed. Lydia's reaction made her stomach twist. How had she been so cavalier in asking Christian to face Bastien, to make such a preposterous request to the man who just learned Christian was his half-brother? She wanted to go to Christian now, to tell him she didn't need this place, that they could create a place of their own.

That he would be her family. But if last night had been any indication, it would be nearly impossible to have a word alone with Luc around.

Lydia pushed open the back door, and they were met with instant warmth from the fireplace near the back entry. Fay worked in the kitchen and the new girl, Edna stood over her, directing. They raised their eyes and greeted Lydia and then Mel.

"Is Bastien here?" Lydia asked, casting a rapid glance at Mel.

Mel caught Lydia's arm. "I have to stop him. He can't ask this. And it isn't just Bastien. He intends to ask Willem too, and Ivete."

Lydia blew through her lips. "If he was hoping to get approval from everyone, he might have started with Ivete. She's the most unpredictable. She might reject his idea."

*My idea*, Mel almost grumbled, but then the other side of Lydia's comment registered. "Would Willem not refuse to have us on this land?"

Lydia laughed. "Willem? I'm sure he'd love to have Christian around."

"Even with..." Her eyes cut to Fay and Edna in the kitchen. They had both paused and were listening to every word without pretense.

"If he's family, all the more reason Willem will want him around. I can't speak for Bastien, but Willem thinks nothing but good of Christian."

Mel swallowed. "He asked me to marry him."

Lydia gave Mel a wide smile, but her eyes showed no surprise. "I couldn't have planned it better myself."

"Did you know?"

Lydia drew a deep breath. "I didn't. I was only tasked with bringing you to the lake, and I didn't quite complete my purpose. I wonder if Christian would have caught you had he not been on a horse."

Mel blushed. She'd run from him like a child in a garden. But when he had caught her she'd been nothing like a child and he more a man than she'd ever known. His strong arms had held her and demanded answers. He wanted her to choose, and no man had asked that of her before. They'd all made choices for her and demanded her obedience.

"I'm glad he caught me." She pressed her knuckles to her cheeks and glanced at Lydia. They must surely be bright red.

"Me too."

# 25

Willem marched to Christian's side and glowered at Luc. "I think you've caused enough trouble. He only means to have a word with Bastien."

Luc didn't take his eyes from Christian. "I'm sure he means more than you could know."

Willem opened his mouth to speak, but Christian put a hand out. No more arguing. He would not ask Willem to choose between his brother and a near stranger. Christian stepped around Luc, but quick as a snake, Luc blocked his path. His hands balled into fists, his knuckles white where the skin pulled tight over them.

Christian straightened his shoulders so he stood at his full height. "I don't have anything to say to you, yet." After all, if Bastien granted him permission and Mel was true to her word, he would have to have a conversation with Luc. The child in Mel's belly would have only one father.

"If you don't, it is because you know you have no ground on which to stand. Leave this place. My father would be disgusted to know the likes of you came here, sullying his name."

A roar burst from Christian, and he shoved at Luc's chest. "He created me! Any shame he has is his own and naught to do with me."

Luc ran at him, slamming into Christian's chest. They hit the ground and Christian's lungs stopped working, but his fists knew just what to do. He hadn't wanted it to come to this, but since it had, he wasn't about to be bested. He hit Luc in the nose, the gut. And he swallowed a curse as Luc's fists rained punches everywhere.

Somewhere, outside of their world of jabs and knocks, Willem yelled. Was Christian supposed to stop? No. Luc wasn't stopping, and neither would Christian. He tugged loose of Luc's hold and shoved to his feet. Luc jumped up and ran at him again, but this time Christian dodged. He swiped at Luc, catching him on the chin. Then strong arms wrapped around Christian's upper arms. "What—" Luc was in front of him with his arms similarly bound by Willem from behind. Christian turned his head. "Bastien. Let me go." Christian sniffed and touched his nose. The tips of his fingers came away bloody.

Luc's eye was already swelling and was bound to be black in the morning.

Bastien leveled Christian with a hard look. "I see you're back."

Christian wiped again at the blood. It ran faster now, but he refused to show any weakness by tilting his head back.

Bastien pulled from his pocket a handkerchief with embroidered trim and handed it to Christian. "You wanted to speak to me?" he said in a low voice.

Christian nodded.

Willem loosened his hold on Luc, instead wrapping an arm around him and guiding him toward the house.

Christian swallowed. Mel was inside that house, and he sent up a silent prayer that she would find the strength to endure Luc while Christian spoke to Bastien about their future.

Christian took the handkerchief away and stared at the bright red splotch—a stain upon something so clean and made with such care.

He met Bastien's stare. "I apologize for bringing such contention upon your family and your land." He used the cloth to wipe the blood from his fingers and shoved it into his pocket. "More so now that I must ask for more."

Bastien kept his gaze trained on Christian but said nothing.

Christian drew a breath for courage. "Mel has agreed to marry me, but she wants to stay here. In Aster Ridge. I wondered if you would allow me to purchase that parcel from the Morrises."

Bastien raised his brows and waited three beats before answering. "The land is not mine. You could buy it from them without my permission."

Christian rolled his shoulders, sore from the beating he'd both given and received. "I don't want to do that. If we stay, I want it to be with your support and that of Willem and Ivete."

Bastien narrowed his eyes. "Has Willem given you his support?"

"I haven't asked him yet. I figure this was your valley first."

Bastien nodded. In agreement or in thought? "You're going to marry her?"

Christian nodded.

"And what of the child?"

"I would raise it as my own. It will be a Milnes." He

met Bastien's eyes, and hoped Bastien understood he was not looking for any handouts because they shared blood.

"And if I decline?"

Christian gulped. "Mel has made it clear she wants to stay here most of all. I would leave for North Carolina without her."

"And when Luc comes to visit?"

Christian wasn't sure which scenario Bastien meant. What would happen when Luc came to visit with Christian here? What would happen with Christian gone? But he knew he wouldn't go that far. If Mel refused to join him east and he couldn't stay in this valley, he would find somewhere else to be. Somewhere close, so that if Mel ever changed her mind she could reach him easily.

"That will be Mel's choice." The adrenaline pulsing through his veins from his encounter with Luc told him his words were a lie. He only prayed Mel would make the right choice, and if she didn't ... well, they would work that out.

"I don't want blood on my grass. I don't want my children seeing grown men fighting, as if it were acceptable."

Christian opened his mouth to speak.

Bastien sliced his hand through the air, quieting him. "But no matter the father, Mel and her child are welcome in this valley. And you."

Christian's throat tightened, at the most unexpected welcome. He'd thought Mel's wish too lofty. He expected to be sent away like a dog begging its master's affection. He was *welcome*? The word sounded foreign as though it didn't mean what he thought. He tried to smile at Bastien. "I didn't mean to bring all this to your yard. I only wanted to ease my curiosity before doing my best to forget the very Graham name."

Bastien chuckled, but the sound weighed heavy. He wasn't yet certain of Christian.

"Thank you. For granting me permission."

Bastien stepped forward and clapped Christian on the back. "Inside to speak with Willem?"

Luc was in there too. And Mel. "Will you keep an eye on Luc while I speak with Ivete? I have a feeling she's the next hardest to win over."

Bastien smiled. "She knows who you are. Willem told her this morning."

Christian nodded and went to the stable for his horse.

He rode hard, burning off a bit of the blood that still pumped from wrestling Luc. He almost laughed to think he'd rued the fact that he'd never wrestled with his brothers. Now he was heading to Ivete's, but not to be her protector. Instead, he would ask if she could stand his presence being permanent.

He threw Blue's reins over the hitching post and jogged up the porch stairs. He knocked three times and heard footfalls inside.

Ivete opened the door, her serene face turned to shock. "Christian what happened to you?" Her hands hovered as though trying to determine what to fix first.

Christian touched his nose. No longer bleeding, but he must look a mess. "I'm fine."

Ivete stepped to the side to let him enter.

He swallowed, his heart still pounding from the gallop, and stepped inside.

"Willem told you, then?" He knew he had, but it seemed too odd to start a conversation counting on someone else having relayed the information.

"That you are my brother? He certainly did."

Brother. Did she consider him such? Perhaps a lady

like her wasn't familiar with the other terms he'd been called. Or perhaps she truly did think of him like that. He brushed the idea away. Better get right to it.

"I'd like to buy the Morrises' land. To stay here in Aster Ridge."

Ivete surveyed him, her chin raised so she looked like a queen placing judgment upon her subjects. "Luc is buying that land for Mel."

"Mel will live there with me. She's agreed to marry me."

Ivete's calm facade broke, and her eyes danced. "She's accepted you?" A half-smile lifted the side of her mouth.

"With contingencies."

Ivete's brows quirked. "Such as..."

"Staying here. She wants to raise her baby here as part of your family."

Ivete blinked, and her head fell slightly to the side. "Our family."

Christian smiled, heartened by her inclusion. "Will you allow me to live in this valley?"

Ivete laughed. "Allow? I know not why you think me in charge of this place. Ask Bastien. Or better, just buy the land from the Morrises."

"I've asked Bastien. I want more than the legal property. I don't want to bring this family any more grief."

"Pfft. The grief will not stop so long as Luc thinks he can get anywhere with Mel. What about the baby?"

"It'll be a Milnes."

Ivete nodded slowly. Then, as though she just remembered his question, she said, "I'll be glad for the company, maybe even glad for the entertainment of watching you best Luc."

"That's not my intent—"

Ivete waved her hand at him. "Oh, stop. I know you mean true. I've seen you watch her. Can't say I blame you. I'm not sure I know a woman who would like to stand next to her for too long." She scrunched up her face. "Too pretty."

She placed her hands on her hips. "Off with you. I guess you'll be seeking Willem's approval next."

Christian nodded, taking her hand between both of his. "Thank you."

She shrugged and took her hand back, but her smile glowed warm. She followed him to the door and shut it behind him. He mounted Blue again and took off, back to Bastien's house, with only one more approval to seek.

He found Willem in the stable, as though he'd been waiting for Christian's return.

Willem's horse was unsaddled and he held a brush in his hand. "Bastien said you might want to speak with me?"

"I'm sure it's no surprise by now. But I want to be sure. How would you feel about Mel and I building on the Morrises' land?"

Willem pushed out his lips, considering the idea. "I'm sure they'll be glad to be rid of the land, though you'll be a terrible neighbor."

Willem's teasing way was familiar to Christian and he smiled. "Would you want us as neighbors?"

"I have a mind to make you sweat as you've clearly decided I'm the easiest of the Grahams, but I'm tired from riding to kingdom come, and I've a passel of guests due back at any moment." He led his horse into the stall and stepped back out, closing it behind him. "I'm sure you're asking as a mere formality as I rode to town and escorted you back. You know I want you for Mel, and if there is any doubt, I apologize. I want you here. I'm glad to know you, and I was sad to think you might go." He stepped closer and nodded at Christian. "Stay. Marry that girl. Have a few kids."

Christian's smile stretched wider than ever. He wasn't sure what he'd expected, but a flame of gratitude grew in his chest. Mel might have wanted to stay for her child, but that baby wouldn't be the only one to benefit from a life here in Aster Ridge. If only Luc would go, or they could build a house overnight and have their privacy.

## 26

———————

Mel was in the kitchen with the three other women. Edna was teaching Fay how to make the thinnest pastry dough Mel had ever seen. She supposed it would be used to make delicate dessert, and if she hadn't just met her man, Mel's mouth might have been watering at the prospect. Despite her heart hammering, her stomach grumbled and Lydia smirked.

"Let's have a bit of lunch, shall we?"

Mel shook her head. "I couldn't eat."

Lydia scrunched her nose. "Let's get you something and we'll just see."

Too soon Mel was sitting at the table with a bowl of stew and a hot roll in front of her. The latch clicked and every woman stopped what she was doing and turned to see who was coming inside.

Willem entered, followed by Luc. Mel's stomach dropped. She gave Lydia a worried glance. She should go out and tell Christian he didn't have to ask everyone for permission to stay. Tell him she'd been selfish and thinking only of her and her baby's needs. Her stomach turned. Her inability to handle confrontation apparently was also an inability to allow others to do it on her behalf.

Luc stepped around Willem and came right to Mel's side. "What does he have to say to *my* brother?"

Lydia strode forward and glared at Luc. "Luc, give her a bit of space."

Luc didn't even glance at Lydia. He had eyes only for Mel. "Where is your gratitude? I could have rejected you any help. I could have sent you somewhere to get rid of the problem. Instead I send you to my family, and you tear it to shreds."

Tears sprang to Mel's eyes, and her throat turned thick. "I—I'm sorry." She hadn't meant to ruin anything for this family. She glanced at Lydia, intending to say sorry to her too. But her friend's eyes were hard on Luc. He continued, "I don't know why I expected anything else. You bloom under attention. You love to please and do as you're told. I guess I should be happy it wasn't Bastien you seduced."

Flames licked at Mel's face and she shot from her chair, her voice low. "I've never seduced anyone."

Luc laughed in her face. "I think those who have met you would say otherwise."

Mel's bottom lip quivered. She dared not look around the space to see if they agreed. It didn't matter. Appearances might say she was some seductress, but those were deceiving. "People might also say *you* are a gentleman. I know you are not." She pointed a finger at his chest. "You deceived me. You played on my uncle's disdain for me. Took advantage of a woman who had no options."

Luc laughed. "You wouldn't know what to do with options. You'd be in a workhouse if it weren't for me sending you here."

She held his gaze. "And I am more appreciative than you know." She wanted to say more, to tell him what this place meant to her, but she refused to sully her longings by telling them to him. "I am not yours. I was never yours. I might have been, yes, if you hadn't been married. As much as I regret that fact, I see now how lucky I am to have not landed as your wife. I pity the woman who has to fight for your affection every day knowing it will be turned the moment you experience a sliver of boredom. I hate that I was that girl, but she is gone now. Changed. And not because of you. You only pushed me further into that submissive woman you described. Christian helped me to fly, to see what life could be."

Luc shook his head. "If you choose him, I will not support you."

At the thought of Christian some of the heat left her face and settled to warm her core.

"And what of my son?"

Mel glanced around the room. "I see no child. The baby I carry is mine. We are unmarried, and you will have no right to the child."

Luc gave the slightest smile as though he were impressed with her knowledge.

She leaned forward, pressing the palms of her hands into the table top. "You believe I cannot think for myself, it is only that I haven't had the need, not until you came and my family rejected me completely."

A look of doubt crossed Luc's face. "I never doubted your ability to think for yourself. I only hadn't seen you find the courage to do it." His words were soft.

Mel swallowed, unsure how to combat this. It was much easier when he was being hateful. "Well, I guess the need for courage came too."

"I'll want to visit my son."

Mel shook her head. "You have no son."

A muscle in Luc's jaw flexed, and the swelling on his eye looked painful. He stepped closer, and Mel had to look up at him. "Just because you found courage doesn't mean you can choose everything. That child has *my* blood."

"He has Graham blood, yes, and so will his father."

Luc fairly growled. He reached out as though to catch Mel. To shake her or embrace her, she did not know.

But she stepped backward, brushing his hands away. "Go to your wife. Make your life there and forget about me."

He stared for a moment, his chin jutting forward. His shoulders moved up with his inhale and back down as he let out the breath. "I'll never take you back."

"I'll never want you back." Mel knew her words didn't hold the same threat, but they were true.

Luc turned and looked at the now empty kitchen. "He leaves you alone when he knows I am inside."

"Should I be afraid of you?"

"*He* should be afraid of leaving you alone with me."

"I think a man should trust the woman he is about to marry." She wanted to smile as she said the words. She wanted to go to Christian's side and hold his hand or let him wrap an arm around her waist and draw her in. "Excuse me." She moved to go around Luc. For a moment she thought he might stop her, but then he let his gaze drop to the ground, and she continued through the kitchen and out the front door.

She hadn't put on her jacket, and the icy wind ran through her clothing as if it weren't even there. Bastien looked up at the sound of the door, and he walked toward her. "Let's go inside. It's too cold out here." His cheeks and nose were red. Christian was nowhere in sight.

Mel turned and stepped back into the warmth of the house. "Where is Christian?"

"Gone to speak with Ivete."

Mel twisted her mouth and glanced at the door, longing to go to him and stop him from risking his heart at her demand. For a rejection from any of these people would be more than a lost plot of land. It would be a rejection of Christian himself.

She faced Bastien. "He's spoken to you?"

"He has."

Mel waited, and when he offered no other revelations, she pried. "And did he ask about anything?"

Bastien stopped removing his boots and raised his eyes to Mel. "I told him he can stay."

Mel's stomach whirled.

Footfalls sounded behind her. "Stay?" Luc's glare switched from Bastien to Mel. "You're not leaving with him?"

Bastien planted his hands on his knees. "Christian wants to buy and build on the Morrises' land."

Luc scoffed. "The land I was going to buy? For her?"

Bastien closed his eyes as though done with Luc's theatrics. Mel was done too. Now that Bastien had approved, Mel felt sure she would get her wish. She was more grateful than ever that Christian had the courage to ask. She wanted to throw her arms around him, to haul him to town for a preacher so she might prove her intent to marry him.

"And how do I fit into this?" Luc asked.

Bastien's face remained stoic. "Exactly as you've always done. At a distance in Chicago."

Luc worked his jaw. "I'm not welcome on my brother's ranch?"

"You are, so long as you behave and stop creating trouble for my family."

"Troub—" Luc pressed his lips into a line. "I'd say the trouble has been all mine."

"Yes, well, keep it in Chicago next time." Bastien glanced at Mel. "Sorry. I didn't mean he shouldn't have sent you here. We have been glad to have you."

"She gets courtesy, and I get coldness. I suppose you'd like me to leave early."

"I don't much care when you go, only that you behave."

Luc threw a glare at Mel and left, slamming the door behind him.

Mel winced and Bastien pressed to standing. "Don't mind him. He's used to getting his way. Always has."

She followed Bastien into the kitchen, which was full once more. He grabbed a bread roll off the counter and bit into it. "I'm going to see if my wife has been able to sleep through all this ruckus. If she has, I'm going to lie down too. Joshua didn't sleep well last night."

Mel looked around and almost laughed. She felt like her life was hanging on a precipice, everything being decided in a single day, and these folks were just living their everyday lives—making food, tending babies. This was to be her life soon. Tears burned her eyes, and she let them fall as she watched this world within the world.

---

CHRISTIAN ENTERED the house and found Mel against the wall, trying to stay out of the way. Her position weighed heavy on his heart. Would she ever feel like she belonged? Even here, where she'd been so adamant that she be allowed to stay, she still didn't want to be noticed. She glanced up at his approach, and if he thought his heart had been burdened before, the tears that wet her face made it break apart. He rushed to her and cupped her face, searching her eyes for answers.

She blinked, causing fresh tears to cascade, and tried to look at the ground, but he held her firm.

The bustle of the kitchen went on as though nobody noticed them. Christian led Mel near the fireplace and pressed her into one of the chairs.

He sat on the hearth with his back to the fire and took her hand in both of his. "What is it?"

"It's so silly. I'm not even sad. It's just ... " She waved her hand in the direction of the kitchen. "They're all so happy."

"And you? Are you happy?"

A small cry escaped her lips. "I am. Bastien told me he permitted you and I to stay." Then, as though something just occurred to her, her eyes snapped back to him. "What did Ivete and Willem say? Oh, I'm sorry I made you do that."

Christian chuckled and pressed her fingers to his lips. "I'm not sorry. I want you to always tell me what you want, and I'll do my best to be sure you get it."

"And what about what *you* want?"

He smiled, her fingers still against his lips as he said, "You've promised to marry me. That's all I want."

She surveyed him with a disbelieving look. "You want more. Nobody has everything."

He let his head fall to one side. "I guess you're right. I

would like to get you a kitchen where you can stand without fear of being in anyone's way."

She gave a nervous laugh. "I'm afraid I don't know how to do anything in a kitchen."

He laughed in earnest. "I guess we'll have to hire someone to tend to it."

Maybe Edna would work for them between guests at the ranch. It didn't matter. They would figure it out.

He knelt at her feet. "They've all granted us permission to live here. I will buy the Morrises' land and build you a house. Will you be my wife?"

Her breath left her in a puff and she smiled, nodding.

"Is that a yes? You've left me wondering and waiting before."

"Yes." She laughed.

He raised up, still on his knees and wrapped his arms around her, holding her tight, never wanting to let her far from him again. He wanted to kiss her, but she'd already had so much taken from her on the wings of an empty promise. He wouldn't take anything until he'd proven his complete commitment—until they were married in the sight of God.

He pulled back, using his thumbs to dry her cheeks. "When?"

Her brows knit together. "Today?"

He laughed and glanced out the window. "I think we can make it to Dragonfly Creek before dark, but I doubt there will be a preacher willing to do it on such short notice."

"Let's try."

He narrowed his eyes. She was so determined, so rushed. "Are you afraid I'll change my mind?"

He still held her face, but she looked away, as though afraid to meet his eyes.

"You are." He found his seat on the hearth again. "Why?"

"I've already been so much trouble."

He stopped her. "I don't mind trouble. A bit of work is just what I need."

She smiled, but her eyes were still unsure. "We'll go tonight. We'll beg a preacher for a ceremony. If he needs time, we'll wait in town until he grants it to us." He glanced at the kitchen with the women bustling around one another in preparation for supper. "You'll want a chaperone. Who would you like to accompany us?"

"A chaperone." Mel sniffed. "My reputation is already in shambles."

Christian held her gaze. "It will be as much for your comfort as anyone else's."

Mel watched the kitchen as well. "They're all too busy. I don't want to ask anything of them."

"What about Ivete? I could ask her."

Mel twisted her mouth and Christian supposed Ivete hadn't been the warmest of the women here in Aster Ridge.

"I'd like nothing better than to marry you tonight and ease your mind of any doubts. But we plan to live in this area, and I don't want there to be talk about us when we've just started our life together."

Mel drew in a deep breath and let it out slowly. "If they can do the math, they'll talk."

That wouldn't do. Christian might be raising Luc's child, but he didn't intend for anyone outside this family to know it. "We'll go farther away, to a town where nobody will remember our faces. Besides the Grahams and the Morrises, who's to know we arrived separate, unmarried?"

Mel nodded.

With her approval, Christian stood. "I'll ask and see where we can go."

Christian left the house to find Thomas walking toward him. He smiled and lifted a hand in greeting. Thomas took his hand in a firm grip and smiled. "Congratulations."

Christian grinned. "Thank you. Actually, I'm searching for a preacher, outside of Dragonfly Creek. We don't want lips flapping about how that babe is coming a bit too quickly."

Thomas pulled his brows together in thought. "Aaron and Eloise used a place in Worthington. You could try there."

Christian bobbed his head. He wasn't sure, but they could always continue to the next town, and then the next, until they found someone.

Thomas raised a finger. "Actually, one of the guests said his brother is a member of the clergy. I suppose he might send him a wire, ask him to come."

From Chicago. It would take at least a few days, and Christian would have to make it well worth his time. He nodded. "Will you introduce me?"

Thomas pivoted and led Christian to the bunkhouse. As they walked, Thomas kicked a rock down the path, "If you won't accept the mare as payment, perhaps you'll consider something a bit more practical. The cabin near our house is vacant. You and Mel are welcome to use it for as long as you need."

The offer was worth more than a dozen breeding mares.

# EPILOGUE

Mel stood in her bedroom, staring into the looking glass. She'd donned her palest gown, a muted pink. For the first time, she was grateful her aunt had sent her with all her clothing. The gown had a hat that matched the lace on the collar and sleeves. This might be the last time she could wear it. The corset already pinched her sides. She wondered vaguely if she would be able to wear it again after the baby was born. She hoped so and smiled at her sentimentality.

Lydia knocked and entered before Mel had a chance to answer, as though her knock had been a mere announcement and not a request for permission. "I think the sun has come out just for you. It is bright and beautiful."

Mel glanced at her window. The clouds had lifted, and it was a true spring day. Even birds sang their joy at the warm sun gracing them once again. "Shall we see if we can get a few seeds planted before the ceremony?"

Lydia laughed and waved her away. "I don't think you

should even walk to the *wagon* in that dress." She met Mel's eyes. "You are exquisite."

The compliment warmed her face and traveled down to her navel. "Thank you."

"If your mother was alive, she would be a watering pot, I'm sure." Then Lydia gave a sniff and Mel saw tears rimming her friend's eyes. They both laughed. "Would she have approved of Christian? I suppose she wanted a rich gentleman with a good family."

"He has both of those things."

Lydia scoffed. "I guess you're right."

The Grahams' acceptance of Christian only solidified her desire to stay in this valley. Not only had this family accepted her and her child, they had accepted their half-brother with the same warmth and charity.

Lydia said, "I'm going to go see if they are ready for you."

Fay entered, a shy smile on her face. She stopped and let out a small gasp. "Mel, you are beautiful." She shook her head. "I was wrong to ever think you'd fall in love with Hugh. Christian is the only man who would have ever caught your eye." She winked. "I think Hugh has a chance with Edna."

Mel smirked at Fay's matchmaking habit.

Fay lifted the bundle in her hands. "From my family. My mother made it for Eloise, but she got married so quickly it wasn't ready in time, then she was gone in such a whirlwind Ma didn't think to send it unfinished."

Mel took the package and carefully untied the ribbon. The wrapping fell away to reveal an expertly stitched quilt. The patches were soft as though they'd come from clothing that was well-worn. "I can't take this. It should be your sister's. Why didn't Otto take it with him?"

"He was a lone rider. He didn't have room for such things."

Fay nodded at it. "Ma wants you to have it. I'll suggest she get started on Edna's now."

Mel laughed. "You are always so certain."

Fay shrugged. "I was right about you and Christian. I could be right again."

Mel didn't see why not. Both Edna and Hugh were handsome folks who were of an age for marriage. Hugh might resist on mere principal, though, not wanting to prove his sister right. Mel almost laughed.

Lydia popped her head back into the room. "They're ready when you are." She lifted a brow and leaned in close. "Your man cleans up nicely."

Mel pressed the back of her hand to her mouth, trying to hide her grin. She stepped out into the hallway, followed by Lydia and Fay. As she walked down the hallway, she smiled. Most people she knew married in large and decorated churches. But this hallway was all the aisle she needed.

When she stepped out from the darkened hall, her gaze fell immediately on Christian, his head down as he shifted his boots on the wood floors of the Grahams' dining area. His hair was neatly combed back, not a lock out of place. She thought of that windy day on the hill when he'd proposed marriage. His hair had been disheveled and wild. She guessed hers had been the same. Whether he was tidy or not, she wanted to look on him for the rest of her days.

He raised his face and met her eyes. She held his gaze as she walked, unable to even glance and smile at those who had gathered to support them. She could thank them later. She wanted to remember this moment forever.

When she arrived at his side he took both her hands and stared so openly, her cheeks warmed. She wanted to press her cold fingers to her face, but Christian gave each hand a little squeeze and smiled. The way the corners of his eyes crinkled made Mel want to fall right into his dark blue eyes. They stayed that way, lost in one another, as the preacher spoke the words of the ceremony. When he had finished, Christian released her hands and slid one around her waist. The other hand cupped her head. He paused as though gauging her interest.

Mel waited, watching him pause for her. Nobody had ever waited for her before, not like this. Mel flung her arms around his neck and their lips came together in a kiss that was the answer to every unanswered prayer. It was love and commitment. It was laughter and learning. It was the baby in her belly and more children to come. He was her family now and nothing else mattered.

They broke apart and Christian spun Mel to face the group.

A cheer went up. Mel laughed and tucked herself into Christian's shoulder. He squeezed her close, not because he wanted the glory, but because he somehow knew her mannerisms and their reasons better than she.

As she looked up at him, she felt overwhelming gratitude that he knew her so well and still wanted her. She knew no other man in the world could have done so, because she would have tried her whole life to hide the worst parts of herself. But Christian knew those parts, and still he stood at her side and held her close.

The benefit to having the ceremony in the main house was that nobody had to go far to start the banquet. The women had been glad for the clergyman's few days' delay, for it gave them time to use all of their stores of flour and to kill one of the fat hens. Even Mel had been in the kitchen. The smell of meat no longer soured her stomach, and she found her eyes were often hungrier than her stomach.

Della had Mel and Christian seated at the head of the table, their chairs so close they had to be mindful of their elbows as they ate. But the company was the best she'd ever known. Christian reached down and found her hand where it rested on her leg. He squeezed it, and she thought he might be thinking the same thing.

Soon all the children had scattered and the adults sat back in their seats, some with hands on full bellies, others sipping the cider from their goblets. Della rose and began clearing dishes. Mel stood but when she lifted her plate from the table she found Lydia at her elbow, pulling the dish from her hands. "You'll not work on your wedding day." Lydia leaned back and spoke to Christian. "Take your wife home, sir."

Mel flinched at Lydia's crass words. It was enough that Mel had forgotten herself and been lost in their ceremonial kiss. Now everyone knew just where they were going and why.

Christian stood and offered his hand. She was eternally grateful to find he didn't have even a shadow of a smirk on his face. She stepped around her chair and headed for the hallway to her bedroom. Christian tugged her toward him and murmured, "We moved your things earlier."

Mel blinked at him. The family had certainly thought of everything. She swallowed, unsure why her throat was so dry when she'd been fine just moments ago at the table. He led her through the silent kitchen and Mel didn't dare meet anyone's eyes. She would have continued out the door with her neck flushed with shame until Lydia met her around the corner. Everyone else was out of sight, but Mel knew the wall was no barrier for sound.

Lydia spoke in a low voice. "There's a little something for you on your bed." Mel had no idea what it was, but Lydia's smirk and discretion had Mel guessing it was something to do with the marital bed. Mel had half a mind to run away, but Lydia's hand was warm on Mel's arm. "It's from all of us ladies."

A rush of love coursed through Mel. She swallowed the lump in her throat, her lip quivering with emotion. "Thank you."

And with those words Mel's embarrassment melted away. She leaned into Christian not with humiliation but with love and security. He was taking her to his bed and there was no shame in it. She wasn't anyone's secret any longer. She was a woman loved. By her man and by those around her. Never would she have dreamed of such a life for herself.

When they reached the cabin, Christian pulled her close. "Shall I carry you over the threshold?" Mel recalled her history lesson about this tradition and how it signified the woman being uneager to leave her family and start her new life. She shook her head and instead tugged him through the doorway, closing the door behind them. Lanterns had been lit and a bottle of wine stood on the table waiting to be uncorked.

A pile of neatly folded fabric was on the mattress and she walked over. When she held it up, a tumble of fabric fell down. It was a full-length lace nightgown, so thin it would do nothing against the bitter wind that howled beyond the walls of this rustic cabin. This garment wasn't for sleeping, it was for taking off. Mel colored to think of the women in her life discussing this gift, possibly stitching the lace on with giddy laughter on their lips.

Mel chuckled to herself. Here, love wasn't hidden. It wasn't used as a weapon, or trickery. It was given freely and openly.

Christian slid his arms around her waist and nuzzled into her neck, his lips finding the hollow under her ear.

She leaned into him, breathing in his scent. "Is this all a dream?"

"Yes." He murmured in her ear and spun her to face him. His lips found hers and she kissed him fully, without an audience. Only her and him, only their mouths, their hands, their home.

The way Christian loved her was with a slow sweetness that altered everything she knew. This wasn't sinful, it wasn't coarse or lewd.

This was love.

And though there had been a time when she thought her mistakes would determine her future, she couldn't deny the surety that everything was as it should be. That no wrong done could ruin everything. That no matter what life dealt, there was plenty of good out there waiting to be found.

# ALSO BY KATE CONDIE

Want free content and more from Kate Condie? Sign up for her newsletter at www.subscribepage.com/katecondienewsletter or follow her on social media @authorkatecondie

# ACKNOWLEDGMENTS

Thank you to my amazing team. To Michelle for alpha reading and being my brainstorm buddy. To Whitney for developmental and line editing. Thank you to Brittany for copyediting and Beth for Copy/Proof/Formatting. To my betas and proofreaders, Cindy, Taryn, & Ariel. And thank you to all my advanced readers for helping to get this book off the ground on launch day. You are all essential to making this book happen. Huge thanks to all of you!

# ABOUT THE AUTHOR

Kate Condie is a speed talker from Oregon. Reading has been part of her life since childhood, where she devoured everything from mysteries, to classics, to nonfiction—and of course, romance. At first, her writing was purely journal format as she thought writing novels was for the lucky ones. She lives in Utah and spends her days surrounded by mountains with her favorite hunk, their four children and her laptop. In her free time she reads, tries to learn a host of new instruments, binge watches anything by BBC and tries to keep up with Lafayette as she sings the Hamilton soundtrack.

9 798430 762896